CHILDSONG

CHILDSONG

Thor Polson

ATHENA PRESS
LONDON

ISBN 10-digit 1 84401 731 1
ISBN 13-digit 978 84401 731 7

First Published 2007 by
ATHENA PRESS
Queen's House, 2 Holly Road
Twickenham TW1 4EG
United Kingdom

Printed for Athena Press

For R. C. R.

*"Behold the dreamer! Let us slay him
and see what becomes of his dreams."*

Foreword

> If, then, nothing is to be feared in the fact that everything is subject to change, why should anyone take a dim view of the mutability and dissolution of all things? For change occurs in accordance with Nature, and no evil can exist in accordance with Nature.
>
> – Marcus Aurelius in Carnuntum (on the Roman frontier)

I wrote this novel in the early 80s. Briefly, its plot concerns a group of students at a small liberal-arts college in the Midwest who self-destruct in one way or another because of their self-centered, childish, Me-Generation attitude, an attitude which the success-oriented atmosphere at the college does little to improve. The protagonist, Tommy Pendoro, drifts through his first year of college trying to find value in institutional education, and a crisis finally forces him to arrive at a compromise between his ideals and the expectations imposed on him by family and society. The events in the book are linked at every level by various themes and writing styles, including elements of Old English poetry (especially the notion of a wandering bard and the use of alliteration), the problem of religion, and a playful, childlike, and often self-absorbed love of words for their own sake, a quality characteristic of young people in late adolescence and early adulthood.

Although there are many sections and entire chapters written in continuous prose, the novel is meant to be experimental and kaleidoscopic, with all the pieces falling together in the third and fourth chapters. Finally, the title *Childsong* is especially important for understanding what I meant to achieve in writing this. That simple song of wonder is all too easily forgotten as we grow older.

After finishing the novel, I submitted it as an unsolicited manuscript to a large publishing house and a local publisher in Seattle. The larger publisher returned the book unread (along with a list of literary agents), while the second, though interested, had never published a novel and was unwilling to take the risk. I lacked the patience and ego to pursue the matter any further at the time, and the book lay on my shelf for many years. In the meantime, a number of friends well acquainted with the work periodically tried to convince me that I should again attempt to get it published, and after revising it thoroughly I decided to turn to agents as the best way of ensuring that my writing would receive a fair reading. Excerpts from the book were received favorably, though no one was willing to peddle it, and once again my lack of ego, patience, and any connections in the publishing world caused me to set it aside. (Not that I think any less of my writing as a result. Indeed, a quick bit of browsing through the best-selling fiction at any bookstore immediately restores my confidence in my ability to express myself creatively in words.) I was delighted, then, to learn of the existence of Athena Press, to whose entire staff I am enormously grateful.

Unlike many other things that I have written, this novel has not been consigned to Pendoro's "pyre", and I can only hope that you will enjoy reading it as much as I enjoyed writing it.

Königstetten, Austria
Summer, 2006

I

The morning sun threw an intricate gridwork of gold onto the wall beside Clifton's head. He was lying by an open window, and the sun and a cool fall breeze pushed themselves insistently at his long, tousled hair. He could hear the sibilant movement of a rake nearby.

He yawned carefully and examined the ceiling of his room. It was flecked with peeling paint, and its mottled appearance promised leakage in the springtime. The room itself needed a thorough refurbishing, and Clifton suddenly felt very old. He rocked himself off the bed and walked over to the lavatory, where he began to splash his face and upper body with cold water. He hummed softly, occasionally glancing over at the bed.

Well, well, he thought to himself. *Well, well, well.*

Clifton's head swam, and he could taste stale beer on his lips. He regarded the image in the mirror with a smile. He had had a good time. He squeezed a thin ribbon of paste onto his tooth-brush and plunged it into his mouth, scrubbing vigorously. The sharp taste stung his mouth as he moved the brush briskly and mercilessly among teeth and gums.

He had certainly had a good time. Events of the evening past began to acquire a sharper focus as his head cleared. He remembered McDougal pressing up beside him urgently in the pub.

"She'll go for it, Cliffy," he had said, "and there's no doubt."

"Well then, Ian," he had replied. "How about a libation to Bacchus? I anoint you as his high priest." He had then poured his beer over McDougal's head. A brief scuffle had followed in the crowd, with Clifton the easy winner. He had pinned McDougal quickly and, looking down into the ruddy face of his friend, had said laughing:

"Perhaps she will, Mac – perhaps she will. Who's to say?"

He allowed himself another smile in the mirror. His upper body glowed with its brief washing, red and glowing in the chill fall morning. He examined his body with pride, observing the movement of each muscle as he reached for the razor resting on the lavatory. His arms and shoulders bunched and relaxed obediently. Clifton leaned over the basin to lather his face. He felt quite merry.

A good time, such a good time. He chuckled inwardly. *Oh yes.*

He was pleased and even amused because he, Clifton, was the author of a plan well executed, the originator of a plan brought off with fastidiousness, yet with the appropriate amount of alacrity. It had been all too easy – the glances, the subtle gestures, the palaver. All had been planned with great attention given to every detail – the words exchanged, the ideas communicated, the intentions conveyed.

Yes, indeed.

Clifton began shaving great swaths across his coarsely bearded face, the razor moving deftly under the dimpled chin. His mind began to wander again and he cut himself, cursing softly under his breath. He dabbed tentatively at the wound with a wet washcloth and frowned. He threw it back into the basin and continued shaving, watching blood mix with lather.

He thought back to the evening past. The matriculating class had been forced to sit through a dinner which included several key members of the faculty. Clifton, though bored, had assumed an air of polite attentiveness, answering questions as they were put to him and returning questions in such a manner as to keep the lagging conversation alive. He was extremely careful to appear neither deferential nor brash in his responses to his superiors – in this fashion he hoped to impress his audience with his levelheadedness.

During the course of the meal Clifton found that he had been seated next to the dean of students, and he soon found an opportunity to introduce himself. He shook hands gravely with the man, treating their short encounter with a suitable degree of respect. He actually knew very little about decorum, and his actions were governed mostly by instinct. They were faintly exhilarating, these dealings with people in positions of power and money, and Clifton weighed each thought carefully before bringing it forth for acknowledgment and approval. He blushed red with self-esteem as he shoveled a forkful of salad into his mouth – he would do very well.

The meal had continued in silence, interrupted only by some occasional question concerning the operation and maintenance of small colleges. Words were offered and received perfunctorily. Ian McDougal had been seated diagonally across from Clifton so that he faced the dean of students. He had kept silent during most of the meal, though he had smiled broadly during Clifton's brief conversation with the dean. As he boldly turned to speak again, Clifton could see McDougal's face perking up out of the corner of his eye, the canine features frozen like a hound on point.

"I understand that the matriculating class is unusually large this year, sir." The dean looked up from his breaded pork chop and chewed pensively, reflecting on Clifton's simple statement of fact. He was a heavyset man, swollen and shapeless. His clothing fit him tightly, bringing out every bulging contour of a corpulence which seemed to center in his face. The striking feature was a dewlap which hung like a goiter under his jaw. Clifton found himself consciously wrenching his gaze away from the pendulous fold of flesh in order to examine the rest of his face. Two roach-colored eyes stared at him from under a small pair of wire-rimmed glasses. Muttonchops covered the better part of his sagging cheeks, tapering gradually to a balding scalp, bald to an advanced degree. The dean was speaking:

"...expanded our facilities in order to accommodate a larger student body. Enrollment has, unfortunately, been on the decline in recent years, and the admissions office has been hard put to it to find recruiters, much less recruitees. Other small colleges like Flanders are facing similar financial problems. If you include escalating matriculation fees, tuition, and other factors..."

Clifton's head rested listlessly, though not apparently so, on the palm of his hand, and he nodded his assent correctly during the interstices of the dean's drawn-out monologue. The dean paused only for breath. Clifton looked over briefly at McDougal, who had moved a wad of fully chewed peas to the tip of his tongue and was wagging it suggestively in Clifton's direction. Clifton shook his head very slightly, returning his attention to the dean's words, which for some reason had ceased entirely. The hydrocephalic head loomed expectantly before Clifton's eyes:

"Well, Mr. Clifton?"

Clifton turned the faucet handle and washed the lather from his face with handfuls of cold water from the half-filled basin. The water made a pleasant percussive sound as it fell back into the lavatory. Clifton pulled the plug and patted his face with a hand towel. He shivered as a current of cold air moved across his naked legs and torso.

The image in the mirror dominated him: his long, fine hair lay in half-coils on his shoulders and neck while the rest of his body lay bare and exposed to the autumn air. The lines of his face revealed little of his character – the mouth and nose, though prominent, did not present any particularly dominant trait to their beholder, and his eyes were of an ingenuous blue. Clifton smiled and shook his hair, observing its brief undulant luster.

All too easy.

It was an instinct, like a second sense of smell. He had seen her eyes glisten in the pub and had known immediately. The outcome was assured. Clifton stood talking with McDougal and others by the bar, though his mind was not actively engaged in the banter. His eyes met with hers time and time again in the crowded room. McDougal was arguing with a student from another college, whose large eyes and pasty complexion gave him a cadaverous appearance. He was shaking his fist at McDougal:

"…and I for one don't see anything to be gained by continuing this conversation, McDougal!" he was shouting. "Time will tell, as you say, and I daresay it will tell in Bridgewater's favor. We have speed on our side, and we're not cocky bastards – we don't have to be."

"'Cocky bastards,' eh, Billings? 'Time will tell,' eh? Eh?" McDougal mocked the smaller man's high-pitched voice and started to mince around him with one hand on his hip and the other cocked coquettishly behind his head. He began to bat his eyelashes, and laughter rose up around them.

"'Oh, I'll have nothing to do with those Flanders bastards,'" he crooned and pulled the bill of his baseball cap around to the side of his head. "'Time will tell,'" he sang as he mimicked him. Billings appeared to be on the verge of tears. Clifton, irritated by the distraction, pulled McDougal aside.

"So what do you know about that girl over there?" Clifton said, nodding toward the girl who continued to stare brazenly at them.

"Oh, *her*. Hmmm." McDougal smiled wolfishly. "And what's it to you, Cliffy?"

"We've been eyeballing for the past half hour. Quit your games for a moment and tell me about her."

McDougal grinned and leaned closer to Clifton, resting his palm against his friend's ear:

"Goes down like a lead balloon, Cliffy – like a lead balloon. And you're just the fellow."

He met the girl once at the bar and once again as the crowd finally dispersed.

A word or two: that was all that had been necessary.

Far too easy.

Clifton heard the movement of sheets to his side. He glanced over briefly and began to brush his hair in the mirror.

"Good morning," he said.

★ ★ ★ ★ ★

DEAN OF STUDENTS FLAXTON, AN ELDERLY, BALDING man bearing his stern rotundity before him as he lumbered ponderously down a narrow suburban street, paused in front of a trim, box-shaped house and thrust his hand into an empty mailbox. A young boy's head emerged from a window of the house and eyed him questioningly. Dean Flaxton shook his head solemnly. No, there was no mail today, no mail at all. The boy's head disappeared into the house.

He walked up the driveway while assessing the condition of the property in front of him: the lawn was fine, the plumbing had been recently repaired, and even though the house itself needed a bit of paint, it was nevertheless in good condition. Perhaps a realtor would be able to fetch a good price for it. The screen door opened and fell behind him. He laid his satchel carefully on a stool in the hallway and proceeded into the kitchen, where his son sat mouthing a weeping peanut-butter-and-jelly sandwich. He put a kettle of water on to boil and spooned instant coffee and sugar into a chipped mug. The cream would be in the refrigerator behind the pickles.

"How was school?"

"Fine."

"Did you learn anything new today?"

"Nope."

The routine had been established long ago, and it never varied. The pot boiled, and he poured its contents into the coffee mug, watching the vapor rise. He picked up a newspaper from the countertop and sat down at the table across from the boy. His eyes fell on a few headlines but eventually rose to study some random objects covering the table between them. He fingered one nervously.

"Where's your mother?"

"Don't know."

He feigned indifference. But over the rim of the mug he again considered the small boy sitting opposite him and for the thousandth time looked futilely for his own face in the face of his only child.

IAN MCDOUGAL, LAUGHING HYSTERICALLY AND ROCK-ing back and forth on top of a giant ball of snow, leaned forward and showed rolling pointed demon-eyes.

"Did you see the way he ran?" he yelped at his friends rooting in the snow below him. "Did you see the way that sorry son of a bitch ran?"

LIL CHEMISE WINCED AT THE HARSH, UNSHADED sunlight flooding into her bedroom and filling every dusty corner with its severe brightness. The window lay open, and as she watched the threadbare curtains flap in weary spasms she listened to the sounds of children playing in the street below. The rays of light illuminated the entire room – the cracked gilt mirror, several slick stuffed chairs, and a cluttered dresser top. She shook two limp, jeweled arms in the bright autumn air and stretched her body rigid under the heavy covers, yawning loudly. She sat up, and while reaching for a cigarette from the night table she glanced at an overturned clock on the floor.

It was already noon.

PROFESSOR CLIFFORD BONSON STRUCK HIS ALARM clock so sharply that it skidded off the table to the floor, where it continued to ring peevishly. Bonson, throwing sheets and blankets to the side, leaped out of bed and kicked it deftly against the molding, where it lay silently. The sortie had awakened his wife, who now glowered balefully from beneath a headful of curlers and facial cream. Bonson looked at her and glared. Going to a window, he drew aside the blind and stared out into the angry red morning.

IN A BUSY CORRIDOR, PAULA FRANKLIN HURRIED toward her next class. She carried her books smartly against her hips, and as she walked she worked a small piece of chewing gum busily between two rows of capped, cavity-free teeth. Boys passed in the hallway, and she believed that she could sense their approval of her neat, trim figure. She smiled to herself but dared not look up, fearing anything that might seem untoward or unseemly. A hand gripped her elbow.

"Paula!"

Facing her stood Betty Stipps, her roommate, a stout girl with a freckled face and red curls.

"Aren't you in a hurry now!" Betty's face suddenly grew darker, and she looked up and down the corridor before speaking again. "But listen! Wait till you hear this. It's about that bitchy Ruth Hager down the hall – you know, the one that has her nose up in the air all the time? Well, you know that Clifton guy that lives up on the third floor, don't you? Nice hair, football player, a real hunk? Well, I was coming back from the music building last night when…"

RALPH NEWTON, A JANITOR, LAID A PUSHBROOM against the wall of an empty corridor and felt for a cigarette in his coat pocket. Resting his back against the wall, he lit it and looked through the smoky skeins at an old clock halfway up the opposite wall. He stood motionlessly, watching the second hand sweep around and around, counting out the long minutes of the early morning.

Four o'clock, he thought. He lifted the broom slowly away from the wall and pushed it idly down the hallway. *Three more hours.*

THE LARGE, UNCOOKED ROAST LAY ON THE CUTTING-block like an enormous chunk of shapeless red clay. Several yards away, with his chin resting in the palm of his hand, a cook stood contemplating its formless bulk. He had seen many other roasts before, many roasts and steaks and other cuts of meat. He was a cook – it was his job to contemplate large, claylike chunks of meat on a daily basis. In the cafeteria outside he could hear the indistinguishable jabber of students. That was part of his job too – he had listened to their jabbering for close to twenty years.

He shuffled up to the cutting-block and began to season the roast. He filled his hands with spices and watched them in a detached way as they moved adroitly back and forth across the ugly red meat. Yes, he was a good cook, a damned good cook. He picked up the roast and slapped it over loudly to its other side – blood spattered his apron. He repeated the procedure, knowing exactly how much spice to season it with. Too much spice and the students would complain; too little spice and more complaints. He should know. After all, he had worked there for close to twenty years. He snatched a long fork from a nearby table and plunged it into the lifeless beef-flesh. It was ready for the oven.

A SUDDEN GUST OF WIND MADE HIS TEE SHOT TAIL off sharply to the left, and Bradley Landau followed its erratic path with his eyes, cursing. Herbert Munro spoke at his shoulder:

"Tough luck, old boy. Still want to play a dollar a hole? You're taking a considerable trouncing, you know."

Bradley frowned, saying nothing. He stood with his hands in his pockets, watching his friend tee up his ball, and Herbert's club soon rose gracefully to the height of its backswing. As it came down Bradley coughed roughly and watched the ball bounce off a tree into a nearby creek.

"No, a dollar will be just fine, Herbert."

G. SHAPIRO FINESTEIN SAT ALONE ON A STOOL IN A bar which he had labored through his middle age to purchase and make profitable. It was after hours. He rubbed his eyes and looked down at the fat numbers scrawled on the curled yellow ledger pages. He glanced up from the figures to a neat stack of bills beside him and, raising a lukewarm cup of coffee to his lips, drew them toward him. In the early hours of the morning, G. Shapiro Finestein tallied his profits, satisfied that he had finally earned enough money to send all of his children through college. He allowed himself a smile: they would have a better life.

TOMMY PENDORO SAT ON A HARD WOODEN CHAIR in the middle of a vacant room and stared at four blank, peeling walls. He thought of other walls he had seen in the past: the wall of his nursery with its bright meaningless patterns, an ivy-covered brick wall he had seen that very day while walking around campus, the crumbling serried walls of razed buildings. He sat transfixed: after eighteen years, he was finally a weanling, perhaps even a man. He walked to the nearest wall and traced a thin veined crack to the floor with his finger. There were many other rooms like his at the college, all of them closed three-dimensional figures, anonymous hollow boxes holding himself and others at a stultifying spiritual impasse. He opened the door and walked out into the hallway. He would serve his time and get out.

FREDDIE TARN LIKED TO SIT ON A CURB DOWNTOWN and watch the pigeons roost in the rain gutters. He liked the way the sun brought out the green, iridescent plumage on the backs of their necks when they turned their heads. He liked to sit all day and listen to their rustling cooing noises, their scraping rustling cooing. They were such peaceful creatures, the pigeons.

FOR AN INSTANT THE OLD LAMP OUT IN THE hallway cast a very narrow triangle on the floor as the door opened and closed behind him. Below, she could hear his light footfall on the worn wooden steps. His whistle could be heard beneath her window, trailing off to nothing as his footsteps faded down the street. She ran her hands up and down the length of her body again and again. He was so young, so very easily seduced. She relaxed and fixed her unfocused eyes on the door through which he had passed.

And yet so very, very lonely.

JOE FINCH SHOULDERED HIS GUN LIGHTLY. HE HAD walked for miles through the dense underbrush on either side of the railroad tracks without kicking up a single pheasant. He did not really care. He was approaching the college now, and his dog worked in front of him, dodging in and out of sight in the knee-deep brush that ripped and tore at his jeans. It was twilight, and a pleasant fatigue warmed him as he watched the lights in the farmhouses sparkle across the fallow, sleeping fields. It began to snow.

THE RESIDENCE HALL HAD BEEN FULL OF NOISE and bustle all day. Standing by his open window, he could see them scurrying across the grounds with their suitcases and hear them yelling like undisciplined children. He could see blotches of them on the opposite campus playing some absurd, sophomoric game with a large rubber ball. It was most disturbing. Their behavior was improper and their energies unchanneled. This incoming class, like all those before it, would be plunged directly into the midst of blatant decadence. Some would immediately fall prey to the lesser vices around them, and still others would persevere only to succumb to a whore's enticements. They would all find out soon enough.

It was strangely quiet out in the hallway. A light rapping sounded at his door, and he walked across the still, empty room and opened the door cautiously. A youth was bent over double in the doorway, displaying two bare, hairy buttocks. He slammed the door and cringed at the waves of laughter that battered his imperfect seclusion.

TOM ROLFE RESTED HIS FOREHEAD AGAINST A CLOSED textbook in his study carrel. He did not understand the material. He had submitted false information in order to be admitted to the college. He did not understand the material, and he would face academic probation or possible suspension. He would be labeled a fraud, and his life would be ruined.

But now he would sleep.

STEVEN PRENTISS PULLED A DUFFEL BAG AWAY FROM A pile of luggage and hoisted it over his shoulder. He sauntered through the station doors and looked about him, inhaling deeply. He liked the town – perhaps he would be able to make a fresh start. He crossed the street.

SUSAN STROMBERG STAMPED BOOKS AT THE LIBRARY and liked to get very high before she went to work: it made all the little numbers and letters look so funny.

RUTH HAGER NEVER BOTHERED TO LEARN THE MOST rudimentary principles of human compassion.

SETH RITTER ADMIRED HIS REFLECTION IN THE mirror. He was to deliver the sermon that day in the chapel. Many people would be attending. He pulled his tie snugly against his neck. He would shout down fire and brimstone upon them; he would imbue their craven souls with the fear of God. Bony hands straightened crisp, starched lapels. His was the power of the ages – the power to create, the power to destroy. A comb furrowed oily black hair. Legions of the Cross had ravaged nations in the name of the Savior – whole nations had been routed before the inexorable juggernaut of the Holy Scourge.

When he finally donned the sacred vestments of his calling, he felt that divine power inflame every fiber of his being.

CLIFTON STOOD IN A FLANNEL SWEATSHIRT AND shorts in the grass just outside the door of Fowler Hall, throwing a football back and forth with Ian McDougal. But his thoughts were not on football or on the blonde-haired girl sitting in the grass watching him. He desired Ruth Hager, and he was accustomed to having his way. The sharp ball whistled from his hand.

★ ★ ★ ★ ★

Tommy Pendoro sat at his desk, looking out his window at the night. His window commanded a good view of the campus – he could see the globe lamps spaced at regular intervals along the winding walkways and the trees black as iron in the stark lamp-light. A figure approached a distant lamp, and Tommy watched it change from an indistinct brilliance into shadow, observing the metamorphosis with sullen detachment. His imagination reared again, and Tommy bridled it sharply. The figure passed out of his vision into the darkness.

Tommy studied the various paraphernalia covering his desk – the pencil holder, the cheap wind-up clock, and the small study lamp. *Spartan.* His eyes rested finally on the sheet of paper directly before him, partly covered by his hands, which moved aside as he picked up the paper to look more closely at something scrawled in the margin:

> *Vapid vying of vanities,*
> *The priggishness of professors…*

Fustian. A sprig of laurel for the alliterative poet laureate. A hearty round of applause, please.

He crumpled the paper into a crude sphere and aimed it at a metal trash can in the corner of the room. The metal resounded flatly.

Tommy looked out the window again at the night. *No, no time for reflection.* The night leaned against him oppressively. Tommy shook his head violently and opened his desk drawer. He pulled out a fresh sheet of paper and slammed the drawer loudly.

"These are not happy thoughts," she said, waving the poem in his face. The paper fluttered dryly in her grasp, a protean bird with tired wings. "You need to get your head screwed on straight, young man, instead of wasting your time feeling sorry for yourself."

She had left before he could reply.

He laid the paper gently on his desk and drew a large book toward him. *Before I could reply. Scarcely edifying, Mother, scarcely edifying.* "Page 19, problems one through nine. You are dismissed." *Age brings transparency to one's own actions and to others'.* "There will be a short quiz on Friday – be prepared." *Drudgery as a nostrum, with no reflection.* The blank expanse of paper presented a soothing void. *Filio-impiety exhibited in freethinking. Put your shoulder to the yoke, Tommy,* "…and do only parts A and B of problem three."

He had been seated next to a tall, gawking fellow with a maroon sweater and a thin, sallow face whose name also began with a P. They assembled in the hallway and filed into the room in alphabetical order. The desks were carefully arranged so as to form a seemingly limitless number of parallelograms, although Tommy was sure that the number was finite and calculable. A teaching assistant was in temporary charge of the class, and he told them to locate desks corresponding to their student ID numbers. Each student was obliged to fold a rectangle of white cardboard lengthwise and write his or her name on it, facing forward. Tommy bent over his piece, spelling his name slowly and laboriously with the thick black marking pen that had been provided:

When the assistant saw the big shaky lettering, he asked Tommy to make out another one:

"A smartass, huh?" he said under his breath as he gave him a new piece of cardboard. The professor had walked into the classroom and was standing patiently behind the lectern. Tommy simpered his gratitude and received a gratifying scowl in return from the assistant.

The professor identified himself to the class and began his lecture. Minutes passed, and Tommy felt the wash of the flowing monotone slowly beginning to erode his concentration: the characters on the blackboard seemed alien to him, and the pencil felt heavy in his hand. A movement to his side distracted him, and he turned his head.

P. was waving his arm frantically in response to a question regarding the various properties of equality. "P. for 'pedant'," Clifton had later said to Tommy. It became apparent that P. knew a great deal about the matter. Tommy watched the shifting hams and protruding, twitching mouth, and he pursed his lips. P.'s lackluster eyes bore witness to his isolation, his confinement to a myopic world of creased book spines. The voice was impetuous and shrill: "…reflexive, transitive, and symmetric…"

Tommy coughed and began to scribble in his notebook:

The Holy Trinity of Equality…

There was a muted knock at the door. Tommy turned in his chair.

"Come in."

The door opened, and a well-dressed form appeared in the doorway. Tommy's eyes flicked up and down.

"You're Clifton, aren't you? Come in, come in."

Clifton smiled and entered the room. He pulled his arms out of his jacket sleeves and removed his baseball cap; his long hair was swept back in a ponytail.

"I thought I'd come over and go over some of those algebra problems with you, Pendoro," he said, drawing a chair up beside Tommy. Clifton picked a book out of his knapsack. "I'm having a few problems."

He had encountered Clifton briefly after class. The latter had uttered the word "sycophant", nodding toward the gawking student ambling down the corridor away from them, and had then walked on without making further comment.

Clifton.

"I assume that you're referring to problems one through nine on page nineteen, Clifton? Excluding, of course, parts C and D of problem three?" *Turgid, forced. Rein in.*

"Yes. Of course."

Tepid.

"You're from the East Coast?"

Clifton opened his book and looked up at Tommy. His face was inscrutable and fixed.

"Yes. How did you know?"

Because your expression reveals neither warmth nor coldness. Because you condescend in answering a question posed by a Nebraskan. Because there is a grain of truth in every stereotype, even in my Midwestern backwardness.

"Your accent."

"Oh." Clifton paused, extending the awkward lapse. "I guess so. Where are you from, Pendoro?"

Courtesy.

"Omaha."

"Oh yeah? Never been to that part of the country."

He's playing with me, smearing on the bullshit.

They remained silent for a few moments.

"I'm having some trouble with part D, problem three, Pendoro," Clifton said, pushing his book at Tommy. "I was wondering if you could help me." His face was expressionless, revealing nothing.

He'll have me do the entire exercise just to observe me. He smiles behind his eyes, this Clifton.

Steven Prentiss, Tommy's roommate, came in later, drunk. Tommy introduced Clifton and discovered that they were already acquainted.

"Sure, sure," Prentiss suspired – his breath reeked of stale beer, his clothes of sour nicotine. "Yeah, we met today at practice. I'll bet you were a hell of a ball player in high school."

"I did all right, I guess."

Clifton the Modest.

"Yeah? Well, you looked pretty goddamned good out on the field. You put the rest of us to shame."

Prentiss looked down at his feet and shuffled them. The corner of Clifton's lip bent up slightly, and Tommy looked over at his roommate's shoes, their corrugated soles and cat's-cradled laces. Prentiss' eyes darted up:

"Hey, why don't you guys take a break? I've got some beer cooling down in my fridge, and I was going to drink one myself. What do you say?"

Tommy watched Clifton's hands and face.

"It's up to Clifton. I think we've finished most of the problems he was having trouble with."

Clifton's eyes moved over to Tommy's and studied them.

Opaque.

"A beer?" he said. "Sure."

Prentiss' face brightened noticeably. He entered his room and emerged with three cans and a half-deflated football. After distributing the beer, he leaned against the wall near the desk and slid down to the floor with a loud outrush of breath, his cheeks swelling and shrinking. He sighed and opened the can – it cracked and hissed in his thick palms.

"Cold beer," he said. "Nothing beats it." He took a long sip and set the beer beside him on the parquet floor.

Prentiss had arrived at school with a cigarette and a duffel bag. He had been in the navy once, he said. Tommy could still remember him walking into the room on the first day, still remember the swagger and cocksure quality in his voice as he sauntered in, singing loudly to himself. He mostly remembered the cigarette, though – it had stuck to Prentiss' thick lower lip and moved violently up and down as he spoke, distractingly priapic. He had laughed coarsely when Tommy eventually made this observation known to him, saying:

"You should see me smoke a cigar."

It moved so now. The room was dark save for the weak light radiated by Tommy's study lamp. Tommy watched the red tip of Prentiss' cigarette move in the half-light as in his childhood he had watched fireflies dance in the twilight on warm summer evenings. Prentiss was speaking:

"…just full of them. We skipped dinner and headed downtown for beers and babes and when we walked into Florin's the place was full of snatch. One named Lil Chemise of all things came up to me and asked me to buy her a drink and the next thing you know we were slow-dancing, with me copping feels left and right…"

Tommy had turned his chair around completely in order to face his roommate. He let the voice-rhythm and wagging cigarette lull his mind. The beer cooled his throat and hand as earlier tension subsided. His imagination reared again and he relaxed, surrendering to the torrent of images.

"…saw Prof Bonson there with one of the bimbos, some carrot-top with rouge – he just about shit his pants when I said hello to him. So I was sitting there drinking some sickly-sweet concoction that What's-Her-Name had ordered, you see, and I was doing the usual, you know – hands and legs under the table and a shitload of small talk. I could see I had the situation pretty well in hand if you know what I mean so after I got her pretty well plied I more or less led her out of the place by the hand and went out to my car. I loaded her in and we headed to Mollens Park. Holy Jesus, she was really working on me…"

He longed for the night, the coolness – purged of the not-yet, bathed in the not-was. His mind rolled and pitched:

And no thought of the girl. Three blocks east and two north would have brought me to Mollens, and by pressing face to glass I could have observed their arms and sprawling legs made anonymous by beads of condensation on the milky windows. "…Jesus Christ, she was really…" *And the walk back: bracing, with a wisp of cloud crossing the face of the moon, with scraps of leaves whipping the cuffs of my trousers while somewhere behind me his cigarette would be pushing wilfully at the night air in the car, bloated and oblivious to outrage. Outside, the vortices of dervished leafscraps impinging on the thin metal membrane of his car, sinuous and seeking, pelting the glass. And the girl? Christ, she…*

"…Holy Christ, she…"

O Most Holy Christ, I have long since come to doubt You.

Tommy Pendoro sat at his desk, looking out his window at the night.

★ ★ ★ ★ ★

It was almost too brilliant, too splendid a morning. Amos sat in bed with the covers pulled up around his waist and watched the small, neat clusters of students making their way toward the chapel. The sere grass shone flecked and lambent through the sparse branches by his window. It was a beautiful morning, and he was late for church.

The sheets and blankets flew to the foot of the bed as he rose to dress. *Socks shirt tie pants belt shoes vest coat and glasses.* Amos stooped before a tiny shard of glass fixed to the plaster wall and pulled a gap-toothed comb through his hair. *Hurry.* The comb moved quickly – front side side back – and clattered on the porcelain as Amos bolted from the room into the hallway. The steps loomed and passed, dark and diminutive.

He met Ruth Hager at the door and muttered a curt hello, moving past her without looking back.

Beautiful, but a whore. She does like me, however.

The church bells pealed admonishment, and Amos hearkened dutifully.

Walkways wound through the withered grass. Earlier, Amos had found them confusing, but now he delighted in their meandering. His surroundings – the buildings, the trees, even the people – gave off a pleasant glow as if imbued with the spirit of the day, the day of rest and worship. Two young men were throwing a frisbee in the quadrangle: the disc sailed across the sky, and Amos felt it drawing him away with it. A twinge of self-reproach thwarted the impulse, and he continued toward the ringing church bells, frowning.

"Breach of faith," he said to the walkway.

The church itself was an overbearing structure: large and brooding, it reared up and dwarfed the flanking buildings. Amos hastened his step. He could see knots of well-dressed students talking on the steps, which rose up to two ponderous oaken doors leading into the vestibule. He sighted two members of the Christian Fellowship standing at the foot of the steps and walked toward them, waiting politely until they had finished their conversation before speaking:

"Well, good morrow to the both of you! And a fine morning it is indeed."

"Oh, hello, Amos," said the one nearest him, a slight youth with sandy hair. "Yes, it is a fine morning, isn't it? I daresay we haven't many of them left. We'll have a mild winter, God willing."

A titter nearby: the one they call McDougal. The others I don't know very well. Leering fools, blasphemous.

"Yes, God willing…"

Their very presence here is blasphemy.

Amos turned to the other.

"I've heard that you're to deliver the sermon this morning, Ritter."

The other, Seth Ritter, was older than Amos. His hair was thinning, and he had a grayness in his face. The loose vestments brought out the gaunt sternness of his form, the hands gnarled and clasped white against his book of scriptures. His body swayed slightly in the breeze.

"Yes, Kirk, you are correct, absolutely correct," he replied in a thin, wheedling voice. "And I've entitled my sermon 'Delilah' in order to titillate those acquaintances of yours in church this morning." He nodded toward McDougal and the others. "As if they didn't have to come anyway."

Amos could see McDougal's teeth. He had heard.

"But no more of this. Let's go inside." Ritter gripped them by their elbows and guided them toward the open doors and into the hushed interior of the church. The service was beginning.

Amos seated himself quickly and noiselessly in one of the back pews closest to the door he had entered. Closing his eyes, he bent his head in silent prayer:

Holy Jesus, I live in a world full of doubt and waywardness. Every day I meet those who have strayed from the path of righteousness. Oh Father, help me to conquer sin in all its forms, and help me make others aware of their dissipation so that they too might fend off temptation and rejoice in Your glory. I pray in Your name.

Amen.

The organ sounded, and he looked up and about him. People were beginning to stand up, and Amos fumbled at the hymnal in front of him, pulling out his program in order to find the proper hymn number. The congregation was already singing when he finally reached the right page:

> *Satan's thrall will forfeit all*
> *On Man's black day of reckoning…*

He stood to sing. His voice carried out over the worshipers, resonant and laden with jubilation. He felt exultant and full of the Spirit of God:

> *The righteous man will rise and stand*
> *To heed his Master's beckoning.*

The hymn concluded and Amos sat down, flushed with exertion.

Ritter approached the pulpit, mounted the short ladder leading up to the lectern, and halted at the top, looking gravely down at the assemblage below him. The chapel was silent except for an occasional cough or murmur. Papers rattled in his hands, and he spoke:

"Most of you have met me at one time or another, and I have met a good many of you during the course of my tenure here at Flanders, a good many. I have seen classes come and go, matriculate and graduate, and as a Flanders alumnus, I am here today to share an observation with you – in particular, an alarming trend which has only fully manifested itself in recent years."

He leaned his weight against the lectern in a posture exuding sincerity and an unquestioning belief in shared values.

"As you know, this is a co-educational institution, and co-educational by design. While permitting enrollment of women, its founders hoped also to discourage many of the temptations attendant on that practice, namely, fornication and its two concomitants: smoking and drinking. In theory, co-education should not be vitiated by these evils; in practice, however, it *has* been, and to an alarming degree.

"In recent years, Flanders has relaxed its disciplinary controls and has treated violations with much less severity than it has in the past. There have been fewer suspensions and expulsions, fewer examples of credits rescinded due to student improprieties. Monitors were thought to be no longer necessary and were consequently removed from the residence halls eight years ago. Some have claimed that the college has backed away from its traditionally 'martinet' stance on discipline because of enrollment difficulties. That, however, is not the case."

Enraptured, Amos sat.

"Flanders has adopted a more lenient disciplinary policy for the following reason: to allow each student to exercise his right of individual judgment. By leaving resistance to those vices mentioned earlier up to the individual, the college hoped to instill a sense of autonomy in its student body; by removing the imposed restrictions, this institution hoped to create a more liberal atmosphere, an opportunity to distinguish between right and wrong without intervention. In so doing, Flanders College offered the chance to profit by one's own mistakes instead of relying on the judgment of others. It was an experiment, and unfortunately, it seems to be failing."

Ritter pushed himself away from the lectern, taking in his audience in a single sweeping look.

"There is no need to describe specific violations of the college's moral code: those of you who have been reprimanded for their conduct will know to whom I am addressing this sermon. I now offer the story of Delilah as a parallel to the moral crisis existing in our college today."

Coughs, murmurs.

"Samson, as you know, had distinguished himself among his tribe for his many feats of strength against the enemies of his people; his courage was well known. His enemies, the Philistines, feared and hated him, and they wished to bring him to harm. They knew well that none could stand up to his awesome strength, so they decided among themselves to get at him indirectly and by the most insidious means possible: they appealed to his wife, Delilah.

"She did not falter a moment in accepting the bribe offered her by the Philistines. 'Coax him,' they said, 'and find out why his strength is so great and how we can overpower him and bind him helpless, and we will give you eleven hundred shekels of silver.' And she did not hesitate. Going to Samson, she said, 'Tell me why your strength is so great and how you can be bound helpless.'"

Ritter's face, shoulders, and arms moved immediately to imitate, questioningly and intimately gesticulant.

"'Do tell me,' she pleaded. And Samson eluded her wiles, telling her first that he could be rendered helpless by being bound with seven fresh bowstrings. Delilah summoned the Philistines and told them to lie in wait nearby while she bound her husband with the bowstrings brought to her by her husband's enemies. When Delilah had finished binding him and said, 'Samson, the Philistines are upon you,' he snapped the bowstrings apart 'as a strand of tow is snapped when it comes near fire'. Yet he was so entangled in his passion that he was blind to the underlying perniciousness of his wife's games. His covenant with God, the source of his fearsome strength, was weakening.

"Her treachery was nevertheless checked for the moment. Samson was of course unaware of his wife's wicked intentions and continued to humor her, telling her next that if he were bound with new ropes, he would lose his great strength. But again, when she had bound him and cried out, 'The Philistines are upon you,' he easily broke free from his bonds."

Amos heard whispering and turned, seeing McDougal and his roommate talking softly at the end of his pew. Rage and pity rose and clashed inside him.

They were not listening.

"And so on. Samson apparently regarded his wife's efforts to disable him with some amusement, and the game gave his imagination free rein. He told her next to bind him with thread; that too failed. Next he told her to weave his seven locks of hair into a web; that too failed. Delilah, undoubtedly fuming by this point, finally used her last trick – a trick peculiar to her gender and as old as mankind – to betray her husband. She played on Samson's affection for her, saying, 'How can you say you love me when you will not share your secret of strength with me?' Samson, weary and deceived by his wife's false sincerity, relented and broke his covenant with the Lord. 'I am a Nazarite,' he said, 'one favored in God's eyes. My hair is my strength – cut it off, and I will be helpless.'

"And Delilah could see that her husband spoke truly. She lulled him to sleep in her lap, cut off his seven locks, and summoned the Philistines who were lying in wait nearby. When Delilah woke him, shouting, 'Samson, your enemies are upon you,' Samson rose, ready to defend himself against the Philistines. But the Lord had left him. The Philistines fell upon him and gouged his eyes out. And so Samson fell into the hands of his enemies."

McDougal tittered; Amos raged. Ritter preached.

"Samson loses his strength twice in this story – his strength of resolve first, then his actual physical strength. The latter necessarily follows from the former, for by giving in to feminine guile, by breaking his covenant with the Lord, Samson had to accept the consequences for his error in judgment; yielding to his weakness, he had to submit to God's wrath. Left on his own, Samson is at first strong, but he gradually weakens and eventually, it would seem, forgets about his vow to his Creator altogether. And that is precisely where the parallel lies between this story and our present-day situation here at Flanders, a situation which is quite serious, but which is fortunately not yet entirely out of your control.

"I say '*your* control' intentionally. The moral restrictions have been removed from this institution and will never be imposed again – never. It is entirely up to you, as Flanders students, to maintain the high moral caliber which has been so characteristic of students here in the past."

Vehement, articulate, well-meaning. And all they can do is laugh. May God forgive them.

"You, like Samson, possess a sacred trust. And you, like Samson, must learn to protect that trust under morally adverse circumstances. And if you do so, then you, like Samson, will find salvation. For Samson, though sightless and shorn of his strength-giving locks, ultimately redeemed himself in the eyes of his Maker. When the Philistines had gathered together for a great feast, they ordered Samson to be brought before them to make sport of his misery. And Samson, blinded and weakened by his many years of travail, appeared at his captors' behest.

"Leaning against the two pillars which supported the pagan banquet hall, he prayed to God, calling His wrath down upon himself and his hated oppressors. 'Lord God,' he prayed. 'Give me back my strength just this one time, to wreak vengeance but once upon the Philistines for my two eyes.' And God heard his prayer – Samson pulled the building down upon himself and the Philistines in an act of complete and final self-immolation."

Forgive them. And me.

"Moral recourse exists always in the eyes of the Savior. We must all seek the strength of Samson. Amen."

Amos tripped blithely down the concrete steps of the chapel and turned sharply onto the sidewalk leading back to his room. He felt euphoric, though the sensation was tempered somewhat by the indecorous behavior of McDougal and his roommate in the sanctuary. Amos had stayed behind in order to congratulate

Ritter on his excellent sermon, and now, as he walked back toward his room, he began to fear that he had been overly exuberant in his praise: Ritter had received the plaudits mutely, offering only a short thank-you in return. Still, he had felt the necessity somehow to compensate for his hallmates' impropriety. It was all very disturbing.

The throng had dispersed when Amos finally stepped through the large oak doors into the sunlight. He felt confused, and he walked along quickly trying to gather his thoughts. The soles of his leather shoes touched the pavement in soft hisses, and he could see sparrows darting from window to window of a nearby academic building. Amos took comfort in his surroundings. The unkempt grounds moved past him on either side, the grass half green, half brown, half fall, half winter. He watched a group of girls walk by on the opposite side of the street. Their long, nyloned legs scissored gracefully beneath their light wool skirts. Amos shivered.

I will welcome winter.

Ahead, he could see two students lolling idly in the sun, one lying in the grass and the other leaning against a lamppost, talking. He recognized McDougal and slowed, his heart leaping ahead apprehensively.

Turn back and go around? No, they've seen me.

Amos resumed his pace.

I will have to go right through them.

Amos looked straight ahead of him as he reached the pair of young men, McDougal's eyes. *Quickly, quickly: eyes directly in front of you, away from his, shoulders relaxed and arms hanging loosely by your sides, straight through them with no signs of weakness. He preys on weakness.*

"Kirk."

Jackaltalk.

"Oh, hello, Ian. What's going on?"

"Nothing much. Cliffy and I are just out here enjoying the nice day. I daresay we haven't many of them left."

Clifton. That's his name.

"No, no. Not many." Amos beamed. "Did you enjoy Ritter's sermon today? I thought it especially grand, the Delilah parallel and what-all, didn't you?"

"Yeah, Kirk. Grand, most grand." A scowl darkened McDougal's face. His elevated tone mocked Ritter's. "It seems odd to me, however, that our self-appointed shepherd for a day would exclude himself from the flock, especially in light of his less-than-moral activities, if all of the stories floating around about him are true. 'You must learn to protect that sacred trust under morally adverse circumstances.' Christ! Like we should thank him for forgiving us for *our* 'sins' while he wallows in his own, the glib bastard."

Lies. Jackallies.

"You must believe, Ian. You speak as an unbeliever. One must learn to separate the wheat from the chaff. Ritter and men of his faith say one thing and one thing only – the Answer lies in Jesus Christ. You must listen."

A smile played across McDougal's mouth, twisting his lips into a grin:

"So what's the Question?"

Amos looked quickly from McDougal to Clifton, who was staring at his feet and busily rubbing the bridge of his nose between his thumb and forefinger, hiding his smile.

They simply will not listen.

Amos turned abruptly on the ball of his foot and continued on his way. Behind him, he could hear McDougal appealing to his friend:

"Answer to what? What's the Question, for Christ's sake?"

Walking slowly up to his room, he encountered Ruth Hager coming down the stairsteps. Modestly dressed, beautiful, she greeted him:

"Hello, Amos."

She passed, and Amos halfheartedly mounted the half-dozen remaining steps to his floor.

Later, much later, as he lay quietly in the darkness, he heard the churchbells strike midnight and felt the tears rising to soothe him. His chest heaved, and he turned two angry eyes toward the jaundiced moon in the window.

Whore.

★ ★ ★ ★ ★

Steven Prentiss straightened, watching the football fly end-over-end through the uprights at the far end of the field. He jogged slowly to the line of scrimmage and took his stance.

"Hut!"

Steven felt his left hamstring contract tightly, overtightly as he surged across the turf, the pain sharp and defined.

Goddamnit.

Nine steps, ten steps brought him to his defender. White-hot needles of pain shot through the back of his thigh. A well-executed headfake brought him into open field heading toward the sideline.

Throw it, goddamnit. Throw it.

The quarterback, encircled neatly by a wall of defenders, looked at Steven briefly before looking downfield. Steven stopped and limped toward the trainer, watching the ellipsoid nose its way gracefully through the air into Clifton's arms. Clifton raised the ball triumphantly over his head and dashed it to the ground.

The son of a bitch. The cocky bastard.

Steven turned and watched Coach Rodgers approaching in worried strides.

"You OK, Prentiss?"

"No." Steven winced. "I think I pulled my goddamned hamstring."

"Here. Give me your arm."

Steven put his arm across Coach Rodgers' shoulders for support, and they walked to the sideline. Coach Rodgers shouted instructions back over his shoulder to the group of players standing idly in the middle of the field:

"Good work today, boys. Run some wind sprints and grab a shower. I'll see you tomorrow before the game. Get psyched for Bridgewater. This is the big one."

He motioned the trainer over as they sat down on a bench. The trainer, squat and crab-like, scuttled hurriedly toward them and stopped.

"What's wrong, Coach?"

"Prentiss pulled his hamstring. Give me a can of that liniment, then go ahead and start picking up the footballs and equipment off the field."

Standing up, Coach Rodgers asked Steven to roll up his pants and lie face down on the wooden bench. Steven could feel the liniment as it dribbled out onto his leg and the coach's strong calloused hands as they began to work the soreness out of the strained tendon. The smell reached him, oily and sharp.

Clifton.

Lying on the chipped wooden bench, Steven watched the players as they darted back and forth across the gridiron in their bulky uniforms. A ray of sunlight suddenly pierced the haze, illuminating the field and bleachers with its rich brilliance. Full of light, Clifton raced ahead of the others, exultant and young. Steven's heart contracted.

Another time, my friend. Another time.

He brooded, steeping in the heat of his frustration, while Coach Rodgers attempted to console him:

"So what if it *is* against Bridgewater? So what? There'll be plenty more big games in the future – you're only a freshman, after all. Stop stewing. You've done a good job for me this season, and I expect you to do a good job for me next season. With plenty of rest you'll be up and at 'em in no time. Relax."

Coach Rodgers swatted him good-naturedly on the rump.

"Go in and grab a shower. I'll see you tomorrow."

As he walked bandy-legged back to the gymnasium, Steven could still see bodies in flight, with Clifton soaring effortlessly above them all.

* * * * *

"Well, how was it?"

Primping, Ruth Hager stood before the looking glass. Preening, she guided a brush through golden strands. Prattling, Susie Quent lay on the bed, her lips pursed momentarily in two tumid folds of fleshy red.

"Well?"

Smiling, Ruth Hager thought:

Jesus.

Blushing, she regarded her image in the mirror, thinking:

Sweet Jesus Christ.

* * * * *

Master Thomas J. Pendoro ambled, shambled, sidled, lolled, rolled, and bowled his way through corridors slick with wax and thick with students. The exuberant young dilettante looked from side to side and up and down in wonder at the heterogeneity of people and linoleum tiles. Alone, unencumbered, he pressed his way through chattering clusters and the piquant wax smell, flaring his nostrils and whinnying softly to himself in delight.

Well, well. His Eminence the Good Dean Flaxton of Voluminousness nears. And a very good day to you, sir.

"And a very good day to you, sir."

A nod, slight swaying of puppy jowls. And a good long day to your wife's lover, too, Sir Cuckold. Smug bastard. What's this? Bunched clique of comely second-floor girls, saucy wenches. Situation calling for minimal mental strain: hellos, what's-going-ons, light gossip, décolletage inspection, and fantasized arse-squeezings. Go to it, boy.

"Well, good morning, ladies. This is certainly a rare occasion, seeing such lovely creatures as yourselves on this campus. And what, may I ask, brings you to Flanders?"

Giggles, squirmings. Play not the fop. Isn't that Ruth What's-Her-Name standing by the one with the enormous flompers?

"We're going to a physics lecture."

Clifton's girl… Hager she is. Nice hair, green eyes, pug nose, coy smile, full lips, buxom, pert derrière, tapered legs, nicely dressed. And she recognizes me.

"You're Tommy Pendoro, aren't you? Don't you live up on the third floor?"

Communication through ambient chitchat. Yes, yes, one and the same. And you know Clifton.

"Yeah, I live right down the hall from Clifton, with Steve Prentiss. What's the lecture about?"

"'The Mutual Attraction of Inert Bodies'. You should come."

Vulpine vixen eyes flashing in double-entendred doubletalk. A lusty young fleshy thing indeed. I hear Kirk's apeshit over her though decries all doings with women. Cherchez la femme.

"No, no. I'm afraid I can't – I have to prepare for a class this afternoon. The topic does interest me, however."

"Yes, it should be interesting. Oh, I've got to be going, Tommy – it was nice talking with you."

In a sudden hurry to leave. I wonder… ah, it's Clifton Broadshoulders she's caught sight of. No doubt about it – a very nice ass and a real flirt. A holy terror in the sack, I'll wager. Woman manwoe – a perpetual thorn in our sides… but it's time for me to take my leave of these others.

"Bye-bye, ladies. See you soon, I hope."

No answer. Like talking to a bunch of chickens. Cluck cluck.

The indomitable Thomas H. Pendoro walked and talked his way courteously and smoothly out of several ensuing social encounters at various levels of difficulty and hazard. Responses ranged from a curt nod to a sudden effusion of warmth from a janitor who was obviously unaccustomed to contact with the higher beings that surrounded him in his everyday routine. Exhausted, the young academician paused at the head of the stairs to consider his next course of action.

Library no lunch maybe restroom inevitably student union certainly. Off we go.

Decided, confident, T. Howard Pendoro III proceeded on his way with a demeanor corresponding to his enlightened position in society. Mock-serious, foot-loose, the nascent absorber of facts skipped down the linoleum cascade into the foyer and ran through the revolving doors into a fall morning, bearer of light and hope. He walked swiftly toward the student union. Students passed.

Cold-weather clothing not flattering at all – baggy, puffy, disfiguring. Downright ugly.

"Hi."

Funny how society determines ideal traits in women. Some universal, the rest particular. Wonder if there's a universally beautiful woman, excluding particulars of course. Majority of particulars makes most efficacious use of the breeding stock – too many universals, too many left out in the cold. "One man's meat, another man's poison" says Prentiss the Sailorman.

"How are you doing? Beautiful day, isn't it?"

Hideous. A heart of gold probably but ugly as sin. Funny too how that works. Without sex, there is nothing. The ugly have too many particulars, I suppose.

"Hi, Ian."

Grinning fool. Says Hager keeps him awake at night with her

moaning from the next room. Feel sorrier for Kirk, though – only a wall
between them. Vicarious coitus. The days of our youth.

Tommy Pendoro pulled open the double doors of the student
union and stepped inside, feeling the air warm his tingling cheeks.
While taking off his jacket, he turned slowly, taking in his
surroundings in the lobby. A poster caught his eye:

DANCE! DANCE! DANCE! DANCE! DANCE!
SATURDAY AT 9 P.M.
FLANDERS GYMNASIUM
BE THERE OR BE

□

Shit, another dance. I should probably go. Hager's roomie maybe. Stupid
but pretty. Do my heart good. Out to dinner perhaps, the dance then, then
God only knows what afterwards. Like an anchor, McDougal says.

Through another set of doors Tommy could see the cafeteria
line winding in long snakeloops around the tables and handrails.
Waves of food odor confronted him and urged, making his
stomach churn and his bowels rumble. He looked at his watch.

Hour to kill. Might as well.

Thomas "the Intrepid" Pendoro, undaunted and radiant,
entered Flanders College Student Union Cafeteria and stood
patiently at the tail of a sinuous queue.

Slow-mo crack-the-whip with me the loser. Give us this day our daily
glop. Sea of anonymity and an abundance of lassies bejeaned and
besweatered. Only existing element to effect procreation desired – opposite
breeding type for our specious species. Aye, and enter the potential date from
the second floor.

"Well, hello there, second-floor person. What's up?"

Pendoro of the Honeyed Tongue they call me.

"Well, hi! Nothing much. Just waiting for a bite to eat. How
about you?"

Nice breathy stress on every other syllable. I just wonder…

"Oh, the same. Say, I don't believe I know your name yet."

In a delectably demure tone of voice, fluttering her eyelashes in a most coquettish manner, the young maiden made answer:

"My name? Puddin' Tame. Ask me again, and I'll tell you the same."

Oog. Pure corn, and she's effervescing all over me. Should have gone to the library instead.

"Really, now. What's your name?"

"Susie Quent. What's yours?"

"Tommy Pendoro. You're Ruth's roomie, right?"

"In the daytime, at least."

Problems on the home front. Rivalry ribaldry. Envies Ruth's brains maybe. Switch to safer ground.

"What classes are you taking, Susie?"

Buzz.

"I suppose you're busy most of the time, then?"

Buzz.

"How do you like Flanders so far?"

Buzz. Buzz.

"Declared a major perchance?"

Buzz.

"And how are things on the second floor?"

Buzz. Buzz. Buzz. Buzz. Buzz...

Let me see. Plate spoon fork tray napkin.

Buzz...

A nice leafy salad no dessert. Roast beef looks good but lack money. The cook must feel like a real ass wearing that ridiculous chef's chapeau at an institutional dining establishment. Eight hundred gastronomes per meal. Geez.

Buzz...

Let me see. Tumbler milk cup coffee sugar and cashier. Quarter dime nickel penny. Ask and lose her quick.

"Hey, that's great, Susie. Listen, before I forget, there's a dance Saturday night. What say we go out to dinner beforehand, then check it out?"

Pendoro, Thomas Voluble, Esq., Wordsmith and Curator of the English Language.

"That sounds like fun. What time?"

Now. Let's do it now on the cafeteria floor and get it over with.

"How about six?"

"That'll be fine. Where do you want to sit now?"

"Uh, well, I'm afraid I have to eat fast to make my afternoon classes, and I was supposed to meet one of my professors here anyway."

"Really? Who?"

Merciless and indefatigable, the fierce huntress caught sight of her quarry concealed in a thicket of circumlocutions and daubed with thick layers of flattery and unction. Shrieking, the virago drove her steed relentlessly toward the prey.

"Well, uhh…"

She's not that stupid. Rubberneck and stall.

"Let me see… oh, there she is. Over there by the window – Ms. Arenson. Listen, Susie, it was great talking to you, and I'll see you Saturday at six if not before then, OK?"

In her guise of *dea ex machina*, the goddess Arenson intervened, throwing her hands toward the galloping nimroddess. Sir Thomas watched the she-devil's head implode and vanish into the heavens, leaving a void.

Thank God she waved. Thank God she even remembers my face. A close one. An empty seat even.

"See you later, Susie."

Timorous Thomas walked and sat.

"Hello, Ms. Arenson."

"Hi, Tommy."

Glad to see me for some reason. Surprised she remembers my name. One out of hundreds each year, I suppose. Speak, fool.

"Do you eat here often, Ms. Arenson?"

"Almost every day. I enjoy watching the young men come and go. It's very stimulating." She paused. "And please call me Linda."

Finished eating. More than just interested. Linda Arenson, Instructor of English. Have to get more facts from Quidnunc McDougal. She's eyeing me now. Rise to the occasion.

"Uh, Linda, I'm having a bit of a problem with the paper you assigned last week. I was wondering if I could stop by your office one of these days and go over it with you."

She smiles; she knows. It's too obvious.

"I really have to run now, Tommy. I find that a little hard to believe since you write so well – in fact, I've been very impressed with your writing so far. But if you're having problems, just stop by my house some evening, and I'll see what I can do for you. I'm rarely in my office these days. See you in class tomorrow."

Tommy Pendoro watched her gather her things and leave. Enthralled, his eyes followed her all the way out of the cafeteria.

Callipygian, saith Clifton Wordwielder. And a professoress, to boot.

★ ★ ★ ★ ★

I'll be right back.
Mnnn.

(Bed squeak flap flap door squeak flap flap flap McDougal's door squeeeeak. Feet flappity fade-flapping down the hallway.)

SHE:　　　　　　　　Bladderful of beer. The toilet: squat plop void wipe relax. Resentful hairy toes in the next stall. A very strange feeling on this floor. Double standard: he's a stud; I'm a whore. Unfair. Should I wake him?

(Back in bed a few minutes later.)

　　　　　　　　　　Mnnn.
　　　　　　　　　　What are you mnnning about?

(A short foreboding lapse.)

　　　　　　　　　　You drank too much this evening.
　　　　　　　　　　…hmmm?
　　　　　　　　　　I said you drank too much. I'm surprised you're not sick.

SHE:　　　　　　　　Why do I sleep with this guy? Why?

HE:	Brzzzhmnnn… made love tonight? Yeah. Almost fell asleep. Is that what she's bitching about? Far too drunk. Has to have it all the time, I guess. Go to sleep, woman. Sleep… sleeeep…
	I don't even know why you took me to that party. All you did was drink and talk to the guys. If Tommy Pendoro hadn't been there I don't know what I would have done. He didn't seem to be having a good time either. Urgh.
HE:	Let me sleep.
SHE:	My first lover in college – is that the reason? Is that a good reason?
HE:	Whole body numb as hell. Party boring… jocks, jockettes, coaches, all losers. Pendoro? Prentiss there too – hates me now for some reason. Limps around like he's proud of his injury. Covering up his bitterness. Only time we spoke was when he reminded me of my fumble in the third quarter that cost us the game last week. Free beer and too much of it… Did she say "sick"?

(Observe the scholar-athlete's vain attempt to stabilize his rapidly rota-revolving head by placing his hind leg firmly on the parquetry beside the bed.)

	It sure must be convenient having someone come down to your room all the time. Why don't you ever stop by my room to see me? Why must I take all the initiative? Uhnnnn…

(Observe young Clifton's doughy complexion and the incipient signs of sot's friend Nausea.)

...termagant...　　　magantter...　　　gantterma...
termaralph...

SHE:　　　　　　　　Oh, Clifton. I think I love you.

HE:　　　　　　　　Pizza?

(Observe the bacchant's abrupt spasmodic lurching motion from a reclining to a sitting position with cranium and oral cavity in a position fixed though oscillating over the lavatory. Briefly note also the fortuitous propinquity of the vomitorium erst lavatory. Pay particular attention to the abdominal muscles of the reveler, contracting violently in an undulant fashion not at all peculiar to Homo stultus but observed also in certain lesser species. Finally, with reverse peristalsis ongoing and prolonged by repletion, examine the composition of the discharge itself: (1) onions, (2) hamburger, (3) anchovies, (4) pepperoni, (5) green peppers, (6) Canadian bacon, (7) mushrooms, and other components not so easily distinguishable combined with an extremely odoriferous fluid consisting of flat beer commingled with gastric acid.)

　　　　　　　　Urhaaaaaurgh! Bleahhh! Pfttt... fttt...
　　　　　　　　Oh my God!

HE:　　　　　　　　Urhaaaaaurgh! Bleahhh! Pfttt... fttt...

SHE:　　　　　　　Oh my God!

★

　　　Loving Mama held waif-urchin in arms and cradled him. Sick in tummy, Boopums spat up on Dama-Dama. Mommy lovingly wiped Kootie's face with wipe-wipe and patty-pat-patted 'Iddle 'Oot until the Sandman came to sprinkle tiny grains of sleep-dust into the bairn's eyes. Rocking, the suckler sang softly:

> *I met a sailor late last night,*
> *Three years returned from sea.*
> *Said I, "This is the man I'll love,*
> *Though he care not a whit for me."*

★ ★ ★ ★ ★

45

t. t. pendoro, self-limiting yet inexorable young writer of poetry, carped covertly in concentric circles of light candesced by a contiguous candle. Pored parchment lay beneath a poised pen:

Autumn Song

Shadows will rise on the scarred floor and fall,
And they will dance, as leaves do, empty shells
Cupped to hear the song of the Worm
In the sighing of old flesh,
Old men huddled in the barren loins
Of this season, a stillborn season,
       A season of Death.

Lovers too will rise on frayed linen and fall,
And dance, as lovers do, caught fast in timeless
Vignettes of arrested motion and aborted sentiment.

On this night, then, on this night only,
Shelter me again in your falling hair;
Let the leaves fall too from the spare
Contorted branches, and let the season
Mourn its passing alone.

       In the brief joy of our love,
       Let it mourn alone.

"What nonsense!" he announced.

"What horseshit!" he proclaimed.

"What complete and utter drivel!" he declared as he set the tip of the page to the candle flame and fell back into his chair, watching the burning doggerel and feeling the fire of his own mortality consume him flesh and bone, body and soul.

★ ★ ★ ★ ★

(Lights. Applause. Orchestral intro. ANNOUNCER *with tympani crescendo.)*

ANNOUNCER: It's going to be a big, big day with lots of big, big prizes. Now, without further ado, the inimitable Ian McDougal!

(Tulmultuous applause. Enter Master of Ceremonies Ian McDOUGAL *dressed in tuxedo, top hat, dog-leer, diamond cufflinks, and iridescent wingtip shoes.)*

McDOUGAL: Thank you, thank you, one and all. It's certainly an enormous pleasure being here today, and I hope that lots of you will have an opportunity to win win win!

*(*McDOUGAL *smiles. Applause.)*

McDOUGAL: Before we begin, let me briefly explain the rules for the benefit of those unfamiliar with our game. First, I tell a number of incomplete jokes to each contestant. If the contestant is unable to answer the question correctly or fill in the punch line, that lucky dog will be forced to choke down a shot of peppermint schnapps!

(Oohs and appropriate aahs from the AUDIENCE.*)*

McDOUGAL: Once the initial round is completed, two players then go on to the second round, Dog-Eat-Dog. In Dog-Eat-Dog, contestants tell incomplete jokes to each other. The first who falters must pick up hard-boiled eggs with his buttocks for the remainder of the show!

(Catcalls. Whistling and loud belching.)

MCDOUGAL: Then, for the *pièce de résistance*, the single remaining player must pit his wits against Punchinello!

(MCDOUGAL points to a motley-clad dwarf hanging upside down above the stage. Dwarf sneers and froths. Applause.)

MCDOUGAL: In this, the last round, the contestant must again complete the joke or supply a satisfactory answer to a riddle. Prizes are awarded at all levels of competition. Let's begin!

(Eager applause. Grotesque and huge, stagehand DEAN OF STUDENTS FLAXTON crosses the stage in a fig-suit, riding a tricycle. He hands a list of names to Emcee MCDOUGAL, who addresses a question to him as he rides off the stage.)

MCDOUGAL: Hey, Dean! Do you know how a fat man makes love to a fat woman?

DEAN: *(looking back over his shoulder)* No, how?

MCDOUGAL: He rolls her in flour and looks for the wet spots!

AUDIENCE: Yuk yuk. Yuk yuk. Yuk yuk yuk.

(Exit DEAN FLAXTON amid storm of guffaws and derision.)

MCDOUGAL: *(dog-leering)* There's nothing like a good joke to start the show off right, I always say. But hey, I'm ready to play! How 'bout you? *(Looks down at list.)* Let's have these contestants up on stage: the Proletarian, the Patrician, and Everyman; also the Butcher, the Baker, and the Candlestick Maker. Come on down, everyone!

(Lights, fireworks. Orchestra strikes up "Disco Infernal" in a fast 7/8 time. Belly laughs, ballyhoos from the audience. Clouds part and a PILLAR OF

FIRE *is seen shimmying to the music. The six contestants approach and mount the stage, encircling their magniloquent host.)*

MCDOUGAL: Why don't we begin by having all of you introduce yourselves?

PROLETARIAN: I'm the Proletarian.

PATRICIAN: I'm the Patrician.

EVERYMAN: I'm Everyman.

BUTCHER: I'm the Butcher.

BAKER: I'm the Baker.

CANDLESTICK MAKER: And I'm the Candlestick Maker.

AUDIENCE: Clap, clap, clap, clap.

MCDOUGAL: And are you ready to play the game?

ALL: You bet!

MCDOUGAL: Well then, let's start off with the Butcher. Mr. Butcher, an easy one to start out with: Tell me, why did the injury-prone student retire momentarily to his room?

BUTCHER: Why, to fetch three cans of beer for himself and his two "friends".

MCDOUGAL: That is absolutely correct.

AUDIENCE: Har-de-har clap. Clap clap.

(BUTCHER swings a meat cleaver triumphantly over his head.)

MCDOUGAL: Good, good! And now, Mr. Patrician, answer this one: What did the freshman say to the older divinity student upon meeting the latter outside the campus chapel one Sunday morning?

PATRICIAN: Hmmm, let me see…

(Manifest annoyance in the AUDIENCE: *imprecations, oaths, and short diatribes are heard throughout the studio.)*

PATRICIAN: I've got it! The freshman said, "I've heard that you're to deliver the sermon this morning."

MCDOUGAL: That's (ho) right (ha ha)!

AUDIENCE: Ho ho hee. Hee hee ho clap.

MCDOUGAL: Yes, we have some sharp ones today, but can *you,* Mr. Baker *(turning sharply on his heel to face the* BAKER), complete this one? A young man walked into a bar and ordered a beer. Standing near a group of friends, he... Can you finish the joke?

BAKER: Uhhhhhhhhhhhhhhhhhh...

1ST VOICE: Answer!

PUNCHINELLO: *(foaming rabidly at the mouth)* Answer!

BAKER: *(looking appealingly at* MCDOUGAL*)* I'm afraid I don't know the answer.

MCDOUGAL: Too bad! Too, too bad!

(Buzzer sounds. A shot of schnapps is produced which the BAKER *immediately imbibes and regurgitates, much to the* AUDIENCE*'s amusement.)*

AUDIENCE: Bravo! Author! Speech! Encore!

(The BAKER *is escorted off the stage by an irate Bridgewater student to the tune of "Hail to the Chef" in a limping 5/4 time.)*

MCDOUGAL: *(cachinnating intermittently)* And that's how we play our game! *(Turns to the wary* EVERYMAN.*)* So, Mr. Everyman, why did the embryonic man of letters descend the stairs?

(No answer from the bemused EVERYMAN. *Shouts from the* AUDIENCE. *A knowledgeable smile suddenly lights up his face.)*

EVERYMAN:	To get to the student union!
AUDIENCE:	Ha ha ha ha ha ha ha!
McDOUGAL:	Ha ha ha ha ha ha!
EVERYMAN:	Ha ha ha ha ha ha!
PUNCHINELLO:	Ha ha ha ha ha ha!
McDOUGAL:	Let's move quickly to Mr. Proletarian here. Mr. Proletarian: Knock knock.
PROLETARIAN:	Who's there?
McDOUGAL:	*(wryly)* Why don't *you* tell *me*?
PROLETARIAN:	Mollensbird? Mollens Street? Mollenstown?
AUDIENCE:	*(demoniacally swaying)* Amen forever glory the and power the and Kingdom the is Thine for evil from us deliver and…
PUNCHINELLO:	*(hissing)* An auto-da-fe! I demand it! Ignite the heretic!

(Schnapps. A bishop appears stage right and pulls the chastened PROLE-TARIAN offstage with a candy-striped crozier.)

McDOUGAL:	And finally, last but not least, the Candlestick Maker. Answer quickly: Did the mawkish burner-of-poems arrive late for lunch?
CANDLESTICK MAKER:	*(without hesitating)* No, he arrived right on "queue".
AUDIENCE:	*(clapping courteously)* Clap. Clap clap.
McDOUGAL:	We've eliminated two of our six contestants. Let's keep the ball rolling, OK? Say hey, Mr. Butcher, a tougher one for you this time: What did the monotheistic stripling call the co-habitant iconoclasts?

(Expectant hush. PILLAR OF FIRE *bends toward the stage.)*

BUTCHER:	*(stammering)* Pa-pa-pa-pa-pa-pa-pagans? *(Schnapps.)* Wait! Idolaters, maybe? Polytheists?

(Boos and jeers.)

1ST VOICE:	Dullard! Gudgeon! Poltroon!
2ND VOICE:	Eggs! Eggs!

(Exit BUTCHER.*)*

MCDOUGAL:	Three contestants left! Mr. Patrician, what do waffles and leather ellipsoids have in common?
PATRICIAN:	*(smugly)* That's easy. They both come in contact with gridirons.
AUDIENCE:	*(in throes of raillery)* No! No more! Down with punnery and related banalities! Down! Down!

(Refuse and other organic debris, including dead cats, appear at the feet of the PATRICIAN.*)*

MCDOUGAL:	*(casting a baleful glance toward the* PATRICIAN*)* Acceptable, but a cheap one, Mr. Patrician. Beware. *(Addressing* EVERYMAN.*)* Mr. Everyman, did you hear about the leaves?
EVERYMAN:	*(expressionless)* Yes, I heard that they were cupped like empty shells to hear the song of the Worm in the sighing of old flesh.
MCDOUGAL:	That is correct.
AUDIENCE:	Hurrah, Everyman! A laudable rejoinder! Praises to the epitome of universalized Man!

MCDOUGAL: Complete the following quickly, please,
                       Mr. Candlestick Maker: A young narcissist,
                       bending over his lavatory in his quarters
                       late one evening, was heard to say,
                       "Urhaaaaaurgh! Blea…"

CANDLESTICK MAKER: (*nervously*) "…cch?" "…hgack?" "…horg?"

1ST VOICE: Merchant of wax!

2ND VOICE: Shaper of tallow!

3RD VOICE: Death to all wick-menders!

PUNCHINELLO: (*swinging down threateningly toward the
                       discomfited contestant*) Quasi-Promethean!

(*Exit* CANDLESTICK MAKER *with merited celerity and a shot glass full of
peppermint schnapps. Orchestra strikes up "Beer Barrel Polka" in a lilting
waltz time.*)

MCDOUGAL: Congratulations, gentlemen! (*Crosses arms
                       and shakes both men's hands simultaneously.*)
                       Let's begin the second round!

(*Master of Ceremonies Ian* MCDOGGEREL *lopes toward the rear of the stage
on all fours with contestants in tow. Orchestra plays "How Much is That
McDougal in the Window?" in staccato septuplets. Grinning broadly, the
canine emcee halts in front of a large duffel bag and with a low growl directs each
of the contestants to sit facing the other with one arm akimbo and the other
cocked absurdly behind his head.* PILLAR OF FIRE *flickers and flares.*)

AUDIENCE: Delightfully ludicrous! Magnificently
                       absurd!

PILLAR OF FIRE: Pfttt… fttt…

MCDOUGAL: (*on point*) Woof! Grrrrrrrwoof! Ki-yi-yi-
                       yi-yi-yi-yi! Bow-wow! Woof! Woof!

(*Scattered applause.*)

MCDOUGAL: (*extending a forepaw to be shaken by each
                       contestant*) Remember, a rapid succession
                       of questions with no faltering whatsoever.
                       Begin!

PATRICIAN: What did the self-righteous acolyte say to the assembled profligates?

EVERYMAN: "There is no need to describe specific violations of the college's moral code." ...What visual properties do moons and malaria victims share?

PATRICIAN: A peculiar jaundiced appearance, said lunar phenomenon occurring only (and mentioned perforce) under certain atmospheric and spatio-orbital conditions. ...A scholar-athlete sat down to dine. While conversing with a superior, he was able peripherally to discern a dollop of half-masticated food matter on his co-dweller's suggestively wagging tongue. He subsequently...

EVERYMAN: ...became distracted, lost his train of thought, and consequently missed a question posed by his superior concerning enrollment attrition, effecting an immense feeling of embarrassment in the stymied one, disappointment in the corpulent poser of questions, and amusement in the interloper, who immediately averted his gaze and finished chewing as though unaware of his roommate's nonplus. ...What did the self-sequestered celibate call the young woman in the adjoining room?

PATRICIAN: A whore. ...Do contiguous candles candesce in concentric circles, yes or no?

EVERYMAN: Only when placed beside self-limiting yet inexorable young writers of poetry carping covertly...

(Interruption of raucous merriment in the AUDIENCE. *Close-up of* 1ST, 2ND, *and* 3RD VOICES, *who respectively hold hands over eyes, ears, and mouth. Laughter recedes.)*

EVERYMAN: Mr. Patrician, what did the so-called
                 demimondaine think to herself while
                 voiding her bladder?

PATRICIAN: "Double standard: he's a stud; I'm a
                 whore." ...A question regarding various
                 properties of equality invariably elicits in
                 pedants...

EVERYMAN: ...a spasmodic extension and retraction of
                 the forelimb commonly referred to as the
                 "arm".

PUNCHINELLO: *(mordantly)* Oho! How very Oedipuissant,
                 Everyman! A veritable master of repartee
                 he is! *(Motions to figures-in-waiting stage
                 right.)* A crozier for this cretin! Out, out, I
                 say!

AUDIENCE: Chuck chuck chuckle.

EVERYMAN: *(steadfast)* An old tar walks into a lupanar.
                 After imbibing an undetermined number
                 of sickly-sweet potations of questionable
                 quality, the salt, after a brief interlocution
                 with a professor, begins to make his
                 rather blatant intentions known to an
                 anonymous strumpet with luminescent
                 lime-green hair. Says he, "Hey, baby, let's
                 go for a little spin in my convertible."
                 Says she...

PATRICIAN: ..."It's too cold for that tonight. Let's go
                 upstairs instead."

*(Buzzer sounds. Invectives, curses, frenzied denunciation from the
AUDIENCE. A gross of hard-boiled eggs is carried onstage by a cynical,
cigar-smoking sailor with bandy legs.)*

1ST VOICE: Depants the aristocrat!

2ND VOICE: Ungird the philistine!

3RD VOICE: Eggs are too good for him!

(Shackled by his double-knit slacks, the PATRICIAN *hobbles from egg to egg, squatting and standing, squatting and standing.* AUDIENCE *cheers. Streamers and confetti flutter down from the balcony. Bonfires are lit in suitable areas of the studio.* PUNCHINELLO *froths;* PILLAR OF FIRE *does a quick two-step to "Edelweiß".)*

McDOUGAL: Oh lucky day! Oh lucky, lucky day! *(Fawns on* EVERYMAN, *who stoops to scratch him behind his ears.)* Let's go to the final round!

(The cynomorphized emcee leads EVERYMAN *to a rota-revolving bed directly below* PUNCHINELLO, *who is still suspended bat-like above the stage. Trumpet flourish as* EVERYMAN *positions himself on the bed.)*

AUDIENCE: Three cheers for the quintessential Man! Glory to the hypostatic Human!

PUNCHINELLO: *(lowering himself down a chandelier to within a foot of* EVERYMAN's *rota-revolving body. Droplets of vitriol and blood form on the dwarf's lips as he speaks.)* So, Everyman! Riddle me this: Alliteratively speaking, what two actions can be performed by a termagant regarding her image in a mirror?

EVERYMAN: Primping and…

PUNCHINELLO: And? AND?

EVERYMAN: *(confidently)* Prevaricating.

(Screams from the AUDIENCE; *cries for blood.* PUNCHINELLO *looks at* McDOUGAL *who, extending his right forepaw, points his far left claw down toward the stage. Dressing* EVERYMAN *in a gorilla suit and chaining him firmly to the chandelier,* PUNCHINELLO *sets fire to the pseudo-simian and clambers up to the rafters, gnashing his teeth. Above, with maidservant* SUSANNE *at his side, he pulls the chandelier up after him until the burning carcass is suspended halfway between stage and ceiling. An acrid ape-smoke permeates the studio.)*

1ST VOICE:	The only good ape is a dead ape!
2ND VOICE:	A most deservèd conflagration!
3RD VOICE:	Burn, burn, *ignis fatuissime!*
ALL:	Gorilla of my dreams!

(Bansheewailing. Caterwauling. Curtain, temple-torn, closes.)

* * * * *

Between, intricately shaped flakes of snow attached themselves to the windowpane. Outside, traffic passed slowly on icy streets, a cortège for the dying season. Inside, Tommy dined, oblivious to the workings of the outer world. Chewing reflectively, he viewed the restaurant's interior: the swinging kitchen doors, the carpeted floor, the handsomely groomed waiters and waitresses, the variety of diners, the cutlery and dishes of food arranged on the table in front of him, and finally his companion for the evening, Miss Susan Quent, dressed tastefully in a beige sweater and blue jeans to suit the occasion. Resting his eyes idly on the strands of blonde hair covering her right breast, Tommy concentrated on things he heard: the gentle collision of goblets, soft laughter, the wheezing voice of an elderly gentleman seated directly behind him, the imagined sound of snowflakes on glass, and finally the pleasantries, murmured and mellifluous, directed toward him by the voluptuous Miss Susan. Lingering on her words, Tommy touched first the oily skin of his forehead, then the slick room-tempered stem of his wineglass, the coarse fabric of the tablecloth, his recently coiffed hair, the cold greasy handle of his fork, and the unguent palm of Miss Susan's hand. The unmistakeable fragrance of perfume was wafted toward him by a passing waitress. Reveling in its sweetness, Tommy tasted pork.

"You really look nice tonight, Susie – you really do. Where did you get that sweater?"

"Oh, it's just something I ordered from a catalogue before I left for school. I had a feeling that there probably wouldn't be any decent clothing stores in this town." A frown creased her face. "I was right."

"That's too bad, really too bad." He fingered his earlobe as he considered his conversational options, all routine, all equally joy-less. "Where do you come from, Susie?"

"Damascus, Missouri." Susie blushed – her cheeks, rouged and cherubic, glowed crimson in the light of the candle. She lowered her eyes apologetically, coquettishly. "A small town. I was glad to get away from there."

"Why? I like the Midwest."

"Well, I suppose it's OK. It's just that there's so little to do back home." Susie squeezed his hand. "And, well, they're all so... so isolated there, shut up in a little town like that. It's stifling."

Tommy sympathetically hooked her fingers in his own.

"So you went to college, eh? To get away from the small-town boredom?"

"Yeah, I guess so. I was just getting sick of everything: the parents, the high school, the drugstore... and the boys. They all seemed so normal somehow – you know, happy to spend the rest of their lives farming and working in garages. You're not like that, Tommy." She continued to look down.

Tommy licked the souring pork from his lips and widened his gaze to include her entire chest, its concealed sloping charm.

"Clifton talks about you sometimes," she continued, "if and when he decides to stop by and see Ruth." A bilious taint colored her voice at the mention of Clifton's name. "He admires you very much for what you do – the poetry, I mean. He calls you a scop." She lifted her eyes blankly. "What's that?"

Tommy looked at his wineglass and watched its image double as he allowed his eyes to go out of focus. Idly he spoke, running his finger around the rim of the blurred vessel:

"A scop is a bard, a wanderer." He looked into her eyes, feeling foolish. "I don't know. Ask Clifton – he'll tell you."

"What I mean is that you're so *sensitive*. You're not like Clifton, McDougal, or Prentiss. Somehow you remind me of Amos – he's sensitive too. Almost too sensitive, really. He gets hurt a lot, doesn't he?"

"Yes. He does." A car passed outside, throwing slush on bare curbs. "A lot. McDougal rides him constantly, but McDougal is just trying to bring him out of his shell."

"He's so *shy*! I've never met anyone like him." Her eyes roamed, gathering in the restaurant, the passersby, the men. "Why does he stay in his room all day long?"

"I think he feels threatened by the rest of the floor, as if they're there to harm him." Tommy tapped his fingers on his plate. "I think there's something else, though. I've heard that he went to some small, fundamentalist prep school somewhere – he told me himself that there were only twelve people in his graduating class. Throw all of those things together, and you get Amos Kirk, I guess." Tommy smiled. "I honestly think that he's afraid to have fun."

"What does religion have to do with it? I'm a Christian too, and I like to have fun. He obviously has a huge crush on Ruth, and what he really needs is to spend some time with a woman. It'd do him a world of good, I think." Susie clasped his hand tightly in her own and looked up at him. "Don't you?"

Tommy shifted his gaze from chest to eyes, from eyes to chest. He looked nervously at his watch and signaled a waiter:

"We'll take the check, please."

Outside it was snowing, and it began to snow harder as they crossed the street onto the campus. They walked hurriedly, and as the gymnasium came in sight, Tommy reached behind Susie to rest his hand on her opposite hip, drawing her closer to him. They walked quietly, quickly as wet flakes fell thickly on their heads and shoulders. Beside him he could feel her hips' soft rhythm, the gentle contractions of her body through her thick winter coat. A sudden moist gust blew snow in their faces, and they paused in the shelter of a large pine tree. Brought suddenly face-to-face, Tommy locked his mittened hands behind Susie, and they touched lips briefly as the flurry passed. He could feel her breath on his ear as he moved to her neck and chin.

"Stop, Tommy." Her hands seized the hair at the nape of his neck and tugged impetuously. "Stop. Not here."

Tommy withdrew and grabbed her hand.

"Then let's go."

VISION: *Random knots of co-students talking, shouting, laughing, pushing, standing, sitting, dancing, smoking, drinking, walking and, in darker areas of the gymnasium, touching (not immediately visible). The poorly illuminated inanimate contents of the gymnasium – chairs, bleachers, band platform, crêpe paper, balloons, origami swans of different shapes and colors, foil ornaments, a large poster reading* GO FLANDERS BEAT BRIDGEWATER, *tables, cups, a littered wooden floor, basketball goals, and peeling plaster walls. On stage, a five-piece band, the instruments including a piano, an electric bass guitar, a drum set, an alto saxophone, and a voice. Nearer, Amos Kirk obscuring a large portion of the gymnasium, Susan X. (surname momentarily forgotten) with a group including both males and females, faculty and students. Immediately identifiable personal acquaintances: two.*

HEARING: *An irritating din emanating from a complex of speakers and other less familiar public-address equipment positioned on both sides of the platform. Amos Kirk's voice, garbled and indistinguishable from the circumambient noise.*

TOUCH (in sequence): *Susie's hand, Amos Kirk's hand, perceiver's leg, shoulder, scrotum (scratched discreetly through pants pocket), hair, nose, neck, unidentified student's hand, perceiver's nose, cheek, and fingers (slightly greasy).*

SMELL (in sequence): *Perfume, cigarette smoke (salient olfactory impression), marijuana smoke (less noticeable), Amos Kirk's breath.*

TASTE: *Pork. Susie's lips and skin.*

Tommy slapped Amos affably on the shoulder and moved past him to where Susie stood *(his shoes clicked on the sticky gym floor)*. He touched her arm *(strangers' eyes converged on him, the intruder)*. He drew her aside *(strands of very fine hair fell across her face and eyes – she pushed it behind her ears and smiled)*. He kissed her *(not briefly)* and said:

"Let's go to the Fowler party."

Passing Amos, Tommy attempted to link arms with him, shouting, "Let's go back to the hall – there's a party there."

Despondent, Amos remained where he was. Tommy and Susie, a new couple, passed through the gymnasium doors out into the snowstorm.

VISION: *Steps descending to the room proper, wainscot, ornate overhead-light fixtures, bookshelves, wooden chairs, wooden tables, a stereo, lamps, curtains, crêpe-paper festoons, a large poster reading* GO FLANDERS BEAT BRIDGEWATER, *a large keg in the exact center of the lounge. Co-students talking and drinking in small clusters (approximate male-to-female ratio: three to five). Noted temporary absence: Susan X. (surname momentarily forgotten). Number of acquaintances visible: fourteen, viz. Clifton, McDougal, Prentiss, Susan Stromberg, Bradley Landau, Betty Stipps, Tom Rolfe, Herbert Munro, Paula Franklin, Joe Finch, Ruth Hager, and other more peripheral social contacts. Occupying immediate field of vision: Ruth Hager.*

HEARING: *Laughter, relatively unobtrusive background music, talking, metallic pounding (attributed to rapid expansion of steam pipes mounted overhead and parallel to the ceiling), singing. Ruth Hager's voice.*

TOUCH (in sequence): *Susie's hand, perceiver's forehead, Clifton's hand, McDougal's hand, perceiver's scrotum (scratched discreetly through pants pocket), nose, thigh, Prentiss' hand, perceiver's eyebrow, nape (reflectively), scalp, Ruth Hager's hair (extemporaneously).*

SMELL (in sequence): *Smoke. Beer. Ruth Hager's breath. Pizza.*
TASTE: *Beer.*

"Good time, Ruth?"

"I guess." She reconsidered. "No, I guess not." She nodded toward Clifton, McDougal, and the others. "He's been over there in the corner drinking with the guys for hours – it makes me mad." Her lips formed a smile. "But I shouldn't feel sorry for myself. How was your evening with Susie Q.?"

"It was all right. We ate dinner at Jacob's and went to the dance at the gym for a while. It was pretty crowded, so we came here." Tommy nodded toward Clifton. "So they're getting ready for the game tomorrow?"

"They're getting *soused* for the game tomorrow. They've been drinking since seven. I should have gone upstairs a long time ago." Her brows lifted slightly. "Where's Susie now?"

"She went upstairs for some reason. She said she'd be right back down." He looked around him and frowned, draining his beer. "You know, I always feel so out of place at those dances over in the gym. It's always too dark, too noisy, and too crowded. Impossible to talk, so all you can do is slow-dance in the corner." Tommy walked to the keg and returned. "I did see Amos there, however."

"The lure of the flesh. He's as horny as the rest of you."

Tommy laughed. "Yeah, sure. Not like the fairer sex, right?"

"We exist only to satisfy men – without that, there is nothing. We merely endure."

"You're really full of shit sometimes, Ruth."

"I know."

Susie appeared suddenly beside them.

"Have you had fun with Tommy tonight, Susie?" Ruth asked urbanely.

"Oh, we've had a pretty good time, I suppose." She moved to his side. "How about you, Ruthie?"

"OK. I've just been talking to Tommy about your evening. Do you have anything planned for later on, dear?"

Enmity leaped suddenly from Susie's mouth, darting and sharp-tongued: "Why aren't you with Clifton, Hager? Doesn't he want it tonight?"

Ruth smiled placidly.

"He seems to prefer McDougal's company to my own this evening. And one question for you, dear." She smiled mischievously. "How's it fit?"

Mock-jocular Thomas intervened:

"Now, now, ladies. We shan't bicker among ourselves. You should be ashamed."

And as a potential martyr:

"It's certainly not ladylike."

And as a diverter of attention:

"Why, look! Here comes Clifton."

Weaving, Clifton approached and halted beside them, swaying slightly.

"Hey, Pendoro," he slurred thickly. "What the hell's going on?" He pinched Ruth's rump and grinned.

Tommy's heart stopped and lurched into motion again. The stereo speakers hissed as someone switched discs. It suddenly seemed very quiet. Clifton's voice punctured the silence:

"You ready to go yet, Ruthie?" He took her hand and moved to leave, winking slyly at Tommy. "We'll see you later, Pendoro." And over his shoulder:

"You too, Susie Q."

Looking after them, Tommy muttered:

"I don't understand."

The beer had mostly rid him of any remaining inhibitions. Turning to Susie, hands thrust timidly in pockets, he said:

"Well! Have you ever seen my stamp collection?"

VISION: *A streetlamp through half-drawn curtains. A sink, a mirror, a rubber stopper, a narrow glass shelf supporting miscellaneous toilet articles, a large cake of soap, a small towel rack, a plastic tumbler, a dresser, a pewter beer mug, a clock radio, and a radiator. Various articles of clothing including jeans, shirts, belts, coats, socks, shoes, mittens, panties, briefs, and brassiere. Lamplight on linen. Lamplight on ankles, calves, thighs, buttocks, back, arms, and hair of one Susan Q. (complete surname slowly surfacing), freshperson, Flanders College.*

HEARING: *Floor- and wall-filtered music. Snoring in the adjacent room (attributed to co-habitant Steven Prentiss). Snow striking glass (imagined). Woman's breathing.*

TOUCH (in sequence): *Key, doorknob, and dressertop. Perceiver's nose and upper lip. Partner's hair, temples, cheeks, lips, back, neck, shoulder, coat, sweater, pants, and shirt. Perceiver's coat, shirt, shoes, pants, and socks. Partner's brassiere, panties, lips, torso, and buttocks. Wool blankets and linen. Partner's lips, chin, neck, shoulders, breasts, navel, and vagina. Wool against elbows. Partner's hair, flank, and buttock. Floor, faucet handle, warm water, and washcloth. Floor, wool blanket, and linen. Perceiver's right forearm. Headrest facing lamplight. Partner's feet, shins, thighs, vagina, torso, breasts, shoulders, arms, chin, nose, cheek, and hair (simultaneous impression).*

SMELL: *Perfume and flesh. Fish? (comparison suggested earlier by floormate).*

TASTE: *Beer. Skin. Water. Skin.*

THOUGHT (sequential and indiscrete): *…hostility almost unbearable to watch petty rivalry over material advantages though ruth has the edge on her upstairs though maybe not downstairs well certainly see like two tomboys scrapping and scuffling all the time vying for male attention at mutual expense when were not at all worth it and that bastard clifton treating her like shit all the time like nothing more than a slab of meat if i were ruth id tell him to go straight to hell instead of catering to his every* *whim shes probably infatuated with a male that doesnt dote on her constantly lure of the flesh she called it yet here i am instead with her roommate susie q for quem quackenbush quern quastmeyer quince quent thats it silken thighs easier than i had imagined dinner dance party bed banter concerning clothes appearance missouri farmers and mechanics breasts oh jesus what else oh and scops of all things loudmouthed clifton called me sensitive too like amos in the gym the contumelious looker-on though i know he likes me optimum length six to ten minutes foreplay knew i was going to get lucky when she said she enjoyed having a good time beside pine trees in gymnasiums in strangers rooms and here i am sharing the greatest intimacy with someone whose last name ive somehow forgotten again though perhaps shes of the type which feels somehow compelled to dissemble in matters of intellect so as not to frighten men off women hold the wisdom of the ages they say what am i supposed to do now i wonder bardbullshit i gave her cant believe the things i say sometimes prophylactics in pants pocket wallet detached describer of experience destined observer never participant though im probably just an arrogant fool she seems to know exactly what to do follow her lead dont even know this woman violation of innocence and other hackneyed phrases quent thats it susie quent cant feel a goddamned thing with this gardenhose on good prentiss is asleep never hear the end of it oh my god definitely likes it lack of sensitivity best for a woman i suppose prolongation what did the blind man say passing fishmarket hi girls mcdougals stupid jokes could almost envy his total disregard for others opinions sometimes though theres a soft spot in ian the cynic as frustrated idealist hope she doesnt wake prentiss not really what i expected at all much tighter wonder if she knows im a tyro only the second ive bedded believe shes spent and i didnt even better wash myself off it comes surreptitiously disposed of aborted ejaculation shape of condom as a topological problem vestal perhaps though doubt it red bed at night sailors delight says prentiss of the seven seas cant believe what comes out of that guys mouth sometimes first time with didnt even get off tells me about the diaphragm now of all times aha ruths question in the lounge makes sense now oh well double protection against future pendoros thirsty hope she doesnt plan to spend the night never sleep with strangers nice to touch someone sometimes however very warm wool warm when dampened so very warm lamplight on twin moons poet observer of buttocks objectivity a lonely bedfellow indeed oh ruth...*

★ ★ ★ ★ ★

I wasn't going to go. I had a big test in biology the next morning so I was going to study in my room as I should have but I didn't. I went.

I couldn't help myself. I had sat down at my desk and cracked the textbook open to the fifth chapter, getting ready to study. But there was a problem. You see, my chair faces Clifton's wall, and of course when I started looking at the wall I started thinking about Ruth in there every night with that jerk, and then I started thinking about what she would look like without any clothes on. But God fortunately sent me a sign, for when lust began to creep into my heart, I caught sight of the Bible, His Holy Word, on the bookshelf above my desk, and I chastised myself for my wickedness – I pinched my cheek real hard until the pain drew my mind away from thoughts of Clifton's whore. It worked, but it only worked for a little while.

It's like what Grandmother said about growing up. She said, "There's going to come a time when your body's sinful cravings will be almost more than you can bear. Sin takes many forms, and you'll find this to be the most difficult of all to conquer because it is a struggle against yourself, against no one else but you. You'll find yourself to be your own worst enemy. But if you are able to rid yourself of your own selfish concerns and put your complete faith in the good Christ Jesus, you'll be able to purge yourself of base desire in His Holy Fire. And yours shall be the Kingdom."

And I thought of that – I really did. And I remembered a time at Kingspoint when we were all sitting around after somebody's birthday party and somebody turned the light out. Tim Donaldson brought out a Coke bottle and announced that we were going to play spin-the-bottle. I hadn't expected anything like that, of course, and I remember trying to leave, but Donaldson went to the door and told me to sit down, so I did. Donaldson was a jerk, but I went ahead and did what he said anyway to see what would happen. So they started playing, and I was amazed to see how eager all the girls were – the Curse of the Garden, I suppose. It sickened me. I sat on a couch until the bottle finally pointed to me, and I got up to leave again, but Donaldson pushed me down. So they spun it around again, and it pointed to Betsy Barker sitting way off in a corner somewhere. I didn't know what to do when she started walking toward me – I guess I panicked. The next thing I remember was kneeling in the chapel crying like a baby in front of the altar. It was dark and a little spooky in there, but I stayed there a long time asking the Lord to forgive Betsy and Tim and the rest of them. I felt a whole lot better when I left, knowing I had won favor in God's eyes.

I felt that way that night staring at the wall in the dorm, kind of panicky, like I didn't know what to do with my hands, and as always in times of temptation, I took the Bible down from the bookshelf for strength. I read:

> *Thus saith the Lord:*
> *"Your wife shall practice harlotry in the city,*
> *Your sons and your daughters shall fall by the sword,*
> *Your land shall be parceled out by measure,*
> *And you yourself shall die upon alien soil…"*

And I felt the Spirit of God move within me, and I felt my soul uplifted, for I knew that the prophecy of Amos excluded me, his namesake and a strict adherent to the Word. It comforted me, and as I sat down to study again, I felt the Power of God pushing the coarse thoughts out of my mind. It worked.

So I studied for about an hour or two and decided to go take a walk to clear my head a little. I met that guy Clifton out in the hall, and we talked for a second. I don't know what she sees in him. He's an OK guy, I suppose, when he's not with his wicked roommate McDougal, but I can't understand what attracts her to him. He seemed a little more friendly than usual, and when I smelled liquor on his breath, I put an end to that conversation mighty quick, I can tell you. He said that he needed to borrow something called a "bong" from Rolfe, so I let him go.

I could hear music as I walked down the stairs, and I suddenly remembered they were having a party down in the lounge that night for the football team. I stuck my head in the door for a second, but all I could see were football players and a big beer keg sitting in the middle of the room. No wonder they lost to Bridgewater the next day. They never learn.

So I left and started to walk around campus. The weatherman

had predicted snow, and sure enough, as I stepped outside it began to come down in big, thick flakes. Luckily, I had dressed warmly enough so I didn't have to go back in again to change clothes. I could almost imagine Grandmother poking her head out of some dorm window, ordering me to go back inside where it was warm, and I smiled to myself, knowing that I was finally on my own and could do pretty much what suited me.

The campus is about six blocks long and four blocks wide, and it usually takes me about forty-five minutes to walk around the whole thing. When I walk with Pendoro, he always talks about "circumambulating" the campus. It cracks me up – he'll throw in a big word just for the sake of using it, just to hear himself talk. He's a pretty good guy, though, that Pendoro is, not like those jerks he hangs out with. We talk about a lot of things, mostly about our families and home towns. He seems real interested in Kingspoint for some reason – I guess it's because he just went to a regular high school and doesn't know anything about Christian schools.

We talk about Christianity sometimes too, but even though he seems to be listening to me, he never answers. "Jehovah has made even blind stones in the desert weep," I said to him once, and he smiled, but it wasn't like he was making fun of me – it was more like it had triggered an old memory that brought a smile to his face. At least I've planted the Seed of Truth in his mind, which will surely take root someday in the future. He only has to believe.

I was walking by the student union when I remembered the poster I had seen in the lobby there about the dance. By that time it was getting pretty cold and the wind had really kicked up, so I decided to stop by the gym for a moment just to warm up a bit.

It was truly a disgusting spectacle. It looked like a large pre-historic cavern with people resembling their ape "ancestors" cavorting around to primitive rhythms. It was so dark that all I could see were forms out on the gym floor and couples groping at each other with their filthy fingers in the corners. I wanted to see it all, so I started to walk around. They were like animals, the way they were wound around each other – they might as well have been naked for all the grabbing and fondling they were doing. I felt like Moses coming down from the mountain. I wanted to stand up on the platform and shout to them, to warn them of their transgressions against their Lord and Creator. But I knew it wouldn't do any good. I pitied them, yet there was no way to make them aware of their iniquity. It was pathetic.

I had been standing by the dance floor for about fifteen minutes when a woman came to me, asking me to dance. I didn't know what to say to her. I felt like releasing all of the wrath that had been building up inside me, but I knew that anything like that would do no good. My vision blurred, and I turned away from her, walking toward the door. That's when I saw Tommy Pendoro, who was standing all by himself with one of the saddest faces I have ever seen. I suddenly felt very close to him, so I walked over to where he was standing to tell him about my pity and frustration. I thought he would understand.

And I thought he did understand at first. I told him everything, and he seemed to know what I was saying, but when he suddenly went over and grabbed that second-floor wench from a crowd of people, I realized that I might as well have been talking to that wall back in my room. I turned from him and looked at the animals, waiting for him to leave. I didn't even turn around when he tried to take my arm to take me back to Fowler with them. I was glad when he was gone.

I stood there a while longer and went back to Fowler by myself. It was still snowing, and I felt empty all of a sudden, like I was the only person on earth. It was almost a pleasant feeling in a way, especially after all I'd been through in the gym.

I studied late into the night. At about two in the morning I heard Clifton in the next room heaving his guts out. *That poor wretched fool*, I thought to myself. But then I heard Ruth singing some sort of lullaby. Her voice was the only sound in the whole building, and I put down my book to listen.

It was beautiful, like an angel's song.

★ ★ ★ ★ ★

Her skis pushed like slender pistons across the empty countryside. She paused at the crest of a small knoll covered with spindly trees and watched a squirrel leap from limb to limb above her upturned face. It darted and ducked among a fine webbing of twigs and branches and stopped suddenly to look at the intruder below. Chattering, it fled to the upper reaches of the tree and from its elevated sanctuary turned to scold her. Susie smiled and looked around her. The land stretched out in rolling hills and white fields, occasionally punctuated by stands of trees and small farmhouses. Leaving the trail, Susie pushed out into a field and skied toward an old barn in the distance.

She had learned to ski as a child when her parents had decided to give her skis for Christmas. On every Saturday morning after that for almost two months her father would come into her room early to wake her. She would dress quietly in the whiteness of the winter morning, shivering a little in the cold room and thinking of icicles. Downstairs she would find her father bathing his face in the steam from his coffee mug. The cereal box and bowl were always set out for her, and they sat in silence, eating quietly, father and daughter.

The drive out to the golf course was a fairly short one. She would sit in the shelter of her father's big woolen arm draped over and beside her, and she would sit watching the segmented highway stripe go under the car or listen to the radioman talk of things she did not yet understand. If the sun was out, she talked; if not, she grew more reticent. Her father talked very little.

He would help her put on her boots and skis, and Susie re-membered the strong, cold fingers lacing the boots tight and clamping the front soles securely to the wood. She could feel too the thick red beard brushing against her skin as he kissed her and set her down in the snow, giving her some preliminary instruc-tions and telling her not to drift out of sight.

She became progressively better with each outing. Her feel-ings toward their Saturday-morning excursions remained the same: neutral. She felt no pressure to remain out longer than she wished, nor did she feel compelled to ski well in front of her father, who always remained stationed beside the car, smoking a pipe and occasionally calling out instructions to her. The entire experience had a peculiar, empty quality to it – the drive out, the skiing, and the drive home. When she reached the point where she could ski by herself, the trips to the golf course ceased. They never went again.

The barn drew near, decayed and gray as lead. Susie slowed and stopped beside it to rest. The door hung limply on rusted hinges, and Susie sidestepped to have a closer look inside. Through gapped slats in the roof she could see gray light falling weakly on half-discerned farm equipment and bales of hay piled haphazardly at the far end of the barn. Straw covered the hard-packed floor, which smelled faintly of livestock. A thin, twisted piece of rusted wire held the door shut. Stepping out of her bindings, Susie unwound the wire and entered the barn. She sat down on a bale and cautiously began to breathe in the air which smelled like so many thing she had grown up with – horses, hay, dust, and old wood. She leaned her head against a plank and stared out across the fields beyond the swinging barn door.

They had agreed to meet on the levee. Waiting until she was sure her parents were asleep, she rose from her bed fully clothed and tiptoed on bare feet to her bedroom door. She could hear crickets and her father's snoring in the next room, but she paused to make sure. It was a sultry night, and she could feel the moisture in the air clinging to her body and clothes, mixing with the sweat that sprang suddenly to the surface of her skin. In her mind she thought of the long hallway and the winding course she had devised which avoided the creaky floorboards that would alert her parents. The oiled door opened silently, and she stepped out into the hall.

Her feet moved carefully and without error – she had practiced walking across the wooden floor many times and had finally grown accustomed to the feel of each warped board, each small depression against her bare feet. Slowly and cautiously she made her way across the floor and to the stairs at the end of the hallway. She could feel her breasts pushing at her halter-top and her lean, smooth legs rubbing moistly against each other in the summer-night heat. She thought of Joel. When she reached the head of the stairs, she descended quickly. When she reached the porch, she ran.

Joel had first touched her at a dance a month earlier. In the darkness of the dance hall they had swayed slowly together, her head resting against his shoulder. The kiss came as no surprise to her. They embraced, and a new sensation touched her young body. She hugged him harder, allowing the rhythm of their bodies to draw them tightly together.

As a person, Joel had little to offer. He would stop by the house, and they would sit on her porch talking. She was bored almost immediately – he talked only of fast cars and horseplay. His hands interested her the most, the way they brushed softly across her face and hair, the way they stroked and explored. She would sit in silence watching the fireflies and moonlight on the trees, waiting for his hands so she would not have to listen to his words. And when he suggested the barn one night as he was leaving, she agreed without hesitation.

The night was growing cooler as she moved across grass and gravel toward the levee. Beneath her she could feel dewdrops and rock fragments dusty and sharp. The moon filled the branches of a large pine tree on the horizon, and she walked surefooted and quickly, feeling gravel turn to dirt, descending the road to the river bottom and the barn. Her path followed a winding avenue of cornstalks and scrub oak. In the distance an expanse of flat fields lay smooth, hugging the river. Behind her the last houselight sank behind the road.

The land leveled, and the road became deeply rutted. She walked carefully between the ruts, sensing the pale moonlight on the fields beside her, irritated that she could not look around her for fear of twisting her ankle. When she looked up, she could see the distant barn squatting squarely on top of the levee in the shallow twilight. Drawing nearer, she could see Joel.

Bells began to ring far away, and Susie lifted her eyes and gazed through waning daylight in the direction of the campus and chapel. She got up and walked slowly across the barn floor to the swinging door. Bells clamored, echoing across fields of snow.

She had sat on the levee for an hour watching the silver river across fields of wheat and barley, watching wisps of clouds cross the face of the moon, waiting for the touch of his fingertips. Words drifted and died stillborn in the stifling night air. When the hands finally came, she relented entirely, yielding up her childhood to a stranger. In the blackness of the barn, she accepted the passing of years and cursed the emptiness inside her.

The last bell hung heavily in the air as Susie clipped her skis on and leaned into her poles. She glided easily down the hill to the line of trees marking the edge of the field. The light was dying, and it was time to return.

★ ★ ★ ★ ★

- I was a sailor once. He wasn't.

- I smoke ciggies and joints. He smokes neither.

- I come from New Jersey. He comes from Nebraska.

- I get it frequently. He doesn't.

- He says he's a sesquipedalian. I'm not, I'm not even sure what one is, and I really wish he'd shut up with that shit.

- I'm in excellent physical condition. He's not.

- I hate school. He's not sure.

- He likes snow on windowpanes. I don't like snow at all.

- He comes from an upper-middle-class family. I come from a rat-ass poor family.

- I swear constantly. He rarely swears.

- My father was a sailor, like me. His father is a c.p.a.

- He scribbles and burns poems. I don't, and I don't understand why he does.

- He's shy with women. I'm extremely blunt with women, and I'm not choosy. That's why I get it all the time: I play the percentages.

- I plan to be a doctor someday. He doesn't.

- He likes Clifton. I don't.

- I'm a freshman. So is he.

- He skips classes. I don't.

- He spends hours sometimes staring out his window at the campus. I don't.

- I will succeed in life. He may or may not.

- He doesn't have a moustache. I do.

- He laughs to himself sometimes in the middle of the night. I don't, and I wish he'd stop. It drives me up the fucking wall.

- I shower and shave once a day. He doesn't.

- I was injured during a scrimmage. He wasn't.

- He talks to Kirk. I only say hi to him.

- When the mood takes me, I like to drink myself blind. He doesn't.

- I don't play with my food in the cafeteria. He does.

- He mumbles to himself. I don't.

- I enjoy describing my sexploits to him. He listens but never returns the favor.

- He goes for long walks by himself sometimes. I don't.

- He thinks Ian McDougal is funny. I can't stand the asshole.

- I wear boxer shorts. He wears briefs.

- When he's not staring out the window or at a blank sheet of paper, he's out in the hallway shooting the bull with whoever happens to be out there at the time. I don't. I seek my entertainment elsewhere.

- He snores. I don't, or so I'm told.

- I don't attend campus events unless I have to. He goes all the time.

- He went with Clifton and McDougal and erected a huge phallus out of snow in central campus last night. I almost went with them, but I stayed here instead.

- They threw a large metal trash can down the stairs when they got back. I didn't do it, even though they told everyone I had. He thought it was funny. I didn't, and I told him so.

- I'm working on a set of calculus problems. Later I'll go uptown. I couldn't even guess where he is right now.

- I'm a Christian by birth and upbringing. He's a pantheist, whatever that means.

- He laid Susie Quent a month and a half ago. I didn't lay her, and I don't intend to.

- He has some strange notions about life. I don't fully understand his way of thinking.

- I like sports. The only sport he claims he enjoys is nude mud-wrestling.

- He reads books that aren't required and doesn't read books that are. I read only assigned material, and that reluctantly.

- He talks of birds and trees and snow. He fancies himself to be a poet, though he'll deny it flat out when asked about it. I've read some of his stuff, and I think it's mostly bullshit. I'm not a poet, and I don't fancy myself to be one.

- He despises me sometimes for what he thinks I am. I despise myself only for what I'm not.

- But I like Tommy, I really do. And I wish he liked me.

★ ★ ★ ★ ★

Spaced at even intervals, streetlamps marched somberly down the thoroughfare, orbs of light against the starvault. Alone, Thomas Pendoro walked, musing:

> *Roads of men, running skew,*
> *Meeting at infinity;*
> *Born of dust, godless few,*
> *Manchild, how I pity thee!*

Behind pickets, a dog, *amicus generis humani*, ululated:

> *Three-headed Cerberus,*
> *Guardian of Hades,*
> *Inclined to perturb us,*
> *'Specially the ladies.*

Behind lay certainty:

> *Sing "Drink chug-a-lug, drink chug-a-lug,*
> *Drink chug-a-lug, drink chug-a-lug!"*

Here's to Brother Thomas,
Who's here with us now!

Ahead lay surmise:

Tommy and Linda sittin' in a tree,
K – I – S – S – I – N – G.
First comes love, then comes marriage,
Then comes a baby in a baby carriage.

Musing, Thomas Pendoro walked alone and stopped in front of a house. Clouds of vapor rose from his nose and mouth as he looked up at a lamp shining through a frosted double-beveled window on the second floor. A figure passed behind the window. Tommy strolled to the door and opened it, absorbing the warm fusty odor of old wood and stagnant air. To his right he could see a pile of scrap wood; to his left, a row of alphabetized mailboxes. He stood on the landing, feeling keys in one pocket and change in the other. He bent closer to the mailboxes:

Prof. Linda W. Arenson – Box #1

Winifred? Wilma? Winthropina? She's never told me. Spend time with this person and don't even know her full name.

"What's your name?"
"Puddin' Tame."

Susan Q. Conundrum. Can't for the life of me figure out what I did to offend her. Didn't even talk to me the next day when I stopped by her room to say hi. Cold, very cold. Awfully friendly in bed though.
Tommy huddled under the bare light bulb, reading the names under the mailboxes.
Arnold Camden – Box #2. Alice Lundgren – Box #3. What am I waiting for? Bruce Parmenter – Box #4. Always feel out of place here: the light, that Arnold Camden guy always sticking his head out his door whenever I walk in. Suppose it doesn't really matter if it gets out. Two consenting adults. And Prentiss thinks I'm out here for the exercise. Be my common-law wife.

With an about-face, Tommy crossed the landing to the staircase and ascended. He stepped quietly to the door and knocked softly. He waited a few moments and knocked again more loudly:

> *"Wake! For the Sun, who scattered into flight*
> *The Stars before him from the field of Night etc."*

The handle turned, and a figure appeared in the doorway. In the meager light Tommy could see a woman dressed in a nightgown leaning against the doorjamb and holding the doorknob behind her:

> *First I went to England, then I went to France,*
> *And then I saw a woman in her underpants.*

"I can't let you in."

"Why not?"

"I have to grade some essays by tomorrow morning. You should have called me first."

"I thought I'd surprise you."

"You certainly did."

"Aren't you going to let me in?"

"I can't, Tommy. I really can't."

"How about tomorrow night?"

"Call me first. Just call me."

Outside, Tommy backstepped down the sidewalk, squinting at the figure bent over the lamp in the window.

So it was a guy after all. I should have worn my glasses. Nuisance stepping in out of the cold however. Fog up like crazy.

Tommy stepped lightly on a patch of ice and continued in long strides down the street. Houses passed on either side with windows lit, glowing yellow. It was growing late, and Tommy watched the houselights go out one by one.

Flaring and dying. Shouldn't let it bother me I suppose. Never promised me anything though first evening was very promising indeed. Hello how are you trouble with paper come off it Tommy OK you've got me but I just thought well you were right how about a backrub golly Ms. Arenson I mean Linda sure and boom boom boom. Squeaky bed and *baby oil. Fell asleep under her fingers walked into her living room afterwards saw her sitting naked on the couch smoking a clove cigarette reading the Venerable Bede. Must have looked bewildered because she started laughing with her eyes turned off the light again next thing I knew boom boom. All the Anglo-Saxon poetry she gave me to read even tried to get me to learn Old English. Encounter like that exactly what Kirk the hobbledehoy monk needs, bearer of the Book and pre-fab thinking. Came with us when we built that snow phallus not knowing what we were up to thought he was going to defrock himself when he did running away through the snow calling us devil's spawn or some such nonsense. A hard case McDougal said. Declared our room a den of dissipation when he saw Prentiss smoking a doobie in one hand with a beer in the other. Absolutely mortified. Cannabis an acquired taste I guess. That Herbert Munro guy down the hall with a big crate of domestic from his farm yet bowl after bowl with no sensation but a sore throat. Prentiss Munro and Landau pre-this pre-that read "pre-$UCCE$$". Sailor Steve keeps on me for screwing around all the time but who cares? He knows what he can do with himself and his purblind pre-kind.*

My poor, bruised male ego. Alack!

An ice-wraith licked its tongue across Tommy's nape, and he quickened his pace, pulling his collar up around his neck and chin. He came to an intersection and hesitated. Ahead he could see the globe lamps fringing the campus.

Not yet. To Frank's. Heigh-ho the merrio.

He turned and proceeded on his way, suddenly grinning. He winced.

Goddamned lips bleeding. McDougal. Even when he's not here he's trouble the time he cleared his netherthroat at that dinner Prof. Bonson had over at his house for his freshman physics students forced conversation silence during coffee then fwonch flurp just loud enough for me and Landau to hear didn't even look up from his plate picked and blew his nose on my napkin while Bonson and wife in kitchen complete lack of manners and feckless to boot. Gets on Prentiss' nerves only because he's Clifton's roomie worse things in the navy I'm sure. McDougal hung his own out to model for snow-phallus Clifton hit him squarely with snowball and shut him up for once. Two lone gonads melting in the sun the next day girls walking by calling ice-testicles a poor poor snowman then plucked up their chins and departed in a huff when I started laughing. No sense of humor whatsoever these people take themselves far too seriously. Do I? Oneself as the greatest source of amusement and McDougal is one of the few who realize that.

Linda…

Houses and lawns had gradually given way to facades and canopied sidewalks as Tommy passed into the older section of town. Streets seemed to narrow as the buildings rose higher around him. Passing a deep stairwell, he could see an old man with a broad-brimmed felt hat balled up at the foot of the steps in a pool of slush thrown there by passing cars. Vomit trickled from the corner of his moustache, and a cigar lay smoking on his lap.

Me in forty years. Alive alive oh.

Tommy stepped carefully down the glazed steps and shook the old man's shoulder gently.

"Wake up, old-timer. It's cold out here."

The old man stirred, and a sudden gush of vomit covered the front of his coat and sleeve. He groaned and began to shiver violently. Tommy pulled him to his feet and put his hand on the railing.

"Up you go. We'd better get you inside before you freeze to death."

After helping him up the steps, Tommy looked up and down the street. The old man had slipped and fallen, striking his head sharply on the iron railing as he collapsed. There were no pedestrians to be seen. Farther down, the words EAT AT FR   K'S flashed fitfully in pink neon.

Frank's only place open now probably. Looks like he's ready for a cup of hot coffee.

They wove their way toward the bar with Tommy supporting most of the old man's weight on his arm.

Reeks of sterno and whiskey. A drunk and a student of the arts, father and son. How many times have I carried you too, Father? How many times have I watched you drink yourself into oblivion? Better go in through the back.

They zigzagged down an alleyway. The drunken man gurgled unintelligibly. They crashed into garbage cans. Tommy fumbled at a screen-door latch. Inside, music played.

They stumbled through the door into the half-light, and Tommy steered the old man toward a spigot over a bucket riveted crudely to the wall. He turned the cold water on hard and brought the old man gently to his knees with his chin resting on the lip of the bucket.

"Need to make yourself presentable, old father," he said, cupping the drunkard's face with his hand. "Tonight you're to deliver a speech denouncing dipsomania to those assembled in the next room. Snap out of it."

My father who art inebriate. Is plowed and ever shall be.

The old man's body heaved in waves. A thin stream of dark-brown fluid dribbled from his lips. He began to mumble:

"...fuckin' Lonny ditched me... supposed to bring me a fifth at the depot but the bastard ditched me... son of a fuckin' bitch..."

Tommy wiped the rest of the liquid from his mouth and stood him up on his feet. He took the older man's arm in his own and turned him until they were facing the interior room.

"Whatever you do, don't fall down and don't pass out. And don't throw up, or they'll throw you right out into the cold again. Do you understand?"

The old man slobbered.

"OK. Let's go."

They passed through swinging double doors into the bar. With eyes directly in front of him Tommy guided the old man toward a vacant booth. On both sides he could feel the turning heads, the eyes. A short, pale, pig-eyed man with an apron and thick forearms stepped out in front of them, and they stopped.

"What the hell did you bring that drunk back in here for?"

"He was in here before?"

"Yeah, that's Freddie Tarn. I booted him out about an hour ago along with some other scum. They're regulars here, when they can afford it." He pointed at the old man. "He has a nasty habit of puking so I usually get rid of him when I see it coming on."

The old man slumped heavily against Tommy's shoulder, muttering.

"I found him freezing to death outside. I thought I'd bring him inside where it's warm."

"That's no concern of mine. If I took care of every lush that came in here I'd have to start up a goddamned homeless shelter. Get him out of here."

"Look, mister – he was freezing to death. And he has nothing on his stomach now." Tommy looked for the first time at the room – the stools, the stained linoleum, the booths, and finally the long polished surface of the bar itself. "At least let him sit in here a while – you're not too busy."

The bartender blinked pudgy eyes. Absentmindedly he wiped the rim of a glass with his apron hem. His eyes softened, and he leaned toward them slightly. In the background Tommy could hear men shouting for beer.

"OK. But if he so much as drools, he's out of here. And you'll clean up any mess."

"All right, all right." They moved toward a booth. "Could you bring me a draw? And a cup of coffee for the old man too while you're at it? Thanks a lot."

Tommy propped the drunk up between the end of the booth and the wall, and he sat down opposite him. The old man kept sliding off his seat, and Tommy had to keep leaning across the table to reposition him. After the bartender had brought the drinks, Tommy leaned forward with his hands on his chin to study the half-conscious man in front of him.

Funny how much he reminds me of my old man – same color hair, high cheekbones, bulldog jaw, broad nose, creased forehead. And drunk of course. Up to me to take care of him after Mom moved out instead of vice-versa traditional way. Stumbled in night after night in a three-piece so hammered he could barely stand up and me the proxy spouse there to wash him up and put him to bed. Could never read after he got home. And one night he kept saying as I tucked him in don't be like me Tommy you're too sharp Tommy don't end up like me I love you Tommy and me sure sure Papa go to sleep and sitting beside him until he dozed off. Words of love from a wino. And the next day screaming at me hung over as if I had killed his mother or something when we both knew that he was the one who had killed his own mother with his debauches and had almost killed mine.

The old man's hands lay on the table between them – red, cracked, splintered, beaten, weatherworn. They began to move slowly, and his eyes flickered open. They rolled toward Tommy, straining to focus. Tommy's mouth twisted into a halfhearted smile.

"So tell me, old man: What have the years taught *you*?"

The hands contracted suddenly into angry fists.

"That son of a bitch left me out to die. Do you hear me? *He left me out to die goddamnit…*"

★ ★ ★ ★ ★

Quickly rounding the corner of a building in a sleeveless t-shirt at three o'clock on a damp morning, Clifton suddenly came to a complete stop. Two bottles of soda were clenched firmly between the knuckles of one hand, and they rattled faintly in the cold air as he stood looking out over the quadrangle. In the thin light given off by the floodlights fixed to each of the three dormitory walls, he could see a large, shapeless blotch in the very heart of the square. Leaving the bottles on the walkway, he plodded through ankle-deep snow until he reached the verge of a shallow pool. He squatted down and thrust his fingers through the surface of the black water, and when the coldness reached his wrist, he plunged his arm still further into the pool and withdrew a muddy clump of grass. He held it up to one of the floodlights in the distance and watched tiny droplets of water run down to the tips of the roots and drop off into the water at his feet. He put it to his nose and breathed in deeply.

"And not a day too soon," he said, rising and splashing back to the walkway. He picked up the bottles and went inside. Inside it would be warm, like spring.

★ ★ ★ ★ ★

The shears moved like a stork's bill through his father's hair:

Clip. Clip. Clip.

The barber's hands moved like two small red crabs across his father's scalp:

Clip. Clip.

The boy had grown weary of the comic book, and he threw it aside with a tiny grunt of exasperation. He crossed his arms and watched the activity in front of him. His father's eyes were closed; a cigarette dangled loosely from the side of his mouth. The boy began to fidget, and reaching beneath him, he pulled wads of old chewing gum from the bottom of his chair and began to roll them into balls. The barber looked up from his father's hair and shook his head. The shears stopped chattering, and his father opened his eyes.

"What did I tell you about the monkey business, huh?" And as an afterthought: "I'll be finished in a few minutes, and then we can go get an ice cream, OK?" His father leaned back against the barber's chair again, and the cigarette glowed. He closed his eyes.

The boy sat perfectly still for a moment, then he reached inside his coat pocket and pulled out a pack of gum. He liked the uniformity of gum, the mass-produced sameness of each individually wrapped stick. When he had little else to do, he would sometimes pull out the gum just to look at it, to admire its bright colors and foil trim. He held a stick in both hands for a long time before he finally unpeeled it and stuffed it into his mouth. He then turned his attention to his surroundings.

The boy had been to the barbershop so often that he was sure he could find his way around the place in the dark. It was old, the street and the other shops nearby were old, and the barber was old. On one side was a line of chairs with a long cracked mirror over it in which the customers could keep an eye on what the barber was doing to their hair. There were two other barber chairs but only one barber. Scattered throughout the shop were outdated magazines and newspapers. Behind the barber were rows of bottled oils and tonics, some of which probably hadn't been used for years. On the floor were hair clumps of many different shapes, colors, and sizes. It was pleasant sitting in the shop, but it grew wearisome after the first fifteen minutes or so. He had read all the comic books, and the barber was too old to be very interesting.

Today his father was going to sea.

"I thought you get free haircuts in the navy," the boy said to the man in the chair. "How come you always come in here before you go on board?"

The cigarette glowed, and an ash fell to the floor. His father's eyes remained closed.

"Pipe down, will you?" The voice was tolerant. "I'll be through in a minute."

The boy frowned and drew a foot up beside him in the chair to play with the shoelaces. The shears snapped and chattered.

"Crappy weather, John," said the barber. "I'd sure hate to have to ship out in this."

"I've left in worse." The sailor opened one eye and closed it again. "Crappy weather where we're going, too. Norway – six hours of daylight and drizzle. That's if you're topside long enough to enjoy it."

"Sometimes I wish I'd stayed in the navy a little longer. Other times I'm glad I didn't, like today." He stabbed his comb toward the window. "Rough seas, dimwits for shipmates, no women, and a goddamned c.p.o. breathing down your neck all the time." He sighed. "It has its ups and downs, that's for sure."

"Yeah, that's for sure." The sailor opened his eyes and studied his reflection in the cracked mirror. "It's a living at least. It puts food in the boy's mouth here." He nodded at the boy, who looked up from his feet for a moment and then continued to lace and relace his shoes. "It keeps the old lady in curlers."

"Yeah. It does that." The barber's hands stopped moving, and he looked down at the sailor's head as if he were reading a roadmap. The chattering sounded again, and he looked at the boy. "It puts me in mind of a painting I saw at a bazaar the other day. The old lady dragged me down there, and I wasn't too interested, really, until I caught sight of this old painting."

He put his hand to a lather dispenser and dabbed lather behind the sailor's ears. "It was from the whaling days, I guess. It showed this young lady in a long dress on one of those widows' walks they used to build on top of the older houses. Of course the wind was blowing like crazy, and she was looking out to sea, you know, waiting for her husband to come back to port and worrying about him drowning and such." A straight-edged razor slapped against leather.

"What was so peculiar about this painting – and something that would've slipped by me if I hadn't been standing there so long waiting for the wife – was a young man in a top hat standing at the door of the lady's house. You could barely see him. He was in the very corner of the painting and real small, but he was there just the same. It got me to thinking back to my own days in the navy." The razor jerked and flicked behind the sailor's ear. The boy sat up in his chair and looked on with renewed interest.

"I enlisted right after high school. I didn't even give myself time to think of doing anything else – it just seemed like the natural thing to do at the time. I'd also gotten married for one reason or another. I was young, and I figured I could do anything I set my mind to, with plenty of time to do it in. So I went to sea with my wife three months pregnant." The barber's voice was old, made old with the telling of his sea story.

"It worked for a few years – I mean, I thought it worked, but I know now that it really didn't. I was home three months out of twelve to see the wife and kid. I never heard a peep out of her, so you can imagine how surprised I was when I came home one night to an empty house. Not even a note. I still don't know where she is." The razor squirmed.

"I was lost for a while, drinking a lot and doing some thinking. I took an extended furlough to straighten things out as best I could. The idea hit me one night in a gutter somewhere – I figured the best thing I could do was to quit the navy, find another woman, a good woman, and settle down once and for all. And that's exactly what I did – met a little woman at that church around the corner and went to barber school. Best decision I ever made." He wiped behind the ears with a damp towel. "I'm not saying I'm the happiest man in the world, not by a long shot. It's just that I didn't want to make the same mistake twice, if you know what I mean."

The boy thought that his father had fallen asleep. The smoke had continued to curl from the tip of his cigarette, and his hands and feet lay completely still in the chair. The barber leaned poised over his head, waiting.

The seaman opened his eyes again and inhaled the rest of the cigarette down to the filter. He looked at the barber in the mirror, looked at the boy at his feet, and looked at the mist blowing across the street outside.

"How much for the haircut, Harold?"

Gray weather always made the boy think of the sea. As they

walked toward the wharf, he thought about wind throwing coats of ice on huddled men, of sailors blowing warm air through closed red fists and looking out at the blurred line between sky and sea with tired gray eyes. In the winter, when the sleet would batter against his window and the cold would creep into his room through the leaking seams, he would lie awake in the small room and think of his father. Curled in a tight fetal knot, he would watch his breath float out into the bare room and think: *This is how we have it. With his money we live. Somewhere now he's living too, filling up space just as I fill up this narrow bed, room, and house with my own life, with my brothers and sisters who are his too. Is he in a cold bed now thinking of us, or is he warm and laughing in some strange city?*

When his father came home, he never asked and was never told. When he was away, his mother never spoke of the man who had lain beside her in the narrow room next to his own.

But the sea pulled at him. After school, he would often walk down to the docks to watch the ships being loaded and unloaded. He would watch the men in the loading cranes maneuver bulky crates into countless holds and listen to men with faces thick with stubble shout at each other with thick-tongued voices in strange languages. He was sitting on a mooring beside a docked ship one day when a large burly sailor suddenly appeared at the top of the ship's gangway and flew in huge leaping strides down to the dock beside him. Behind them, a group of sailors had gathered at the edge of the ship and were waving their arms in the air and shouting at the burly man standing beside the boy. The sailor laughed and gestured crudely at his shipmates. A large duffel bag flew and landed in a pool of oil at his feet. He stepped forward and snatched it from the ground, growling and cursing at the row of faces laughing and craning out over the water. The sailor turned and saw the boy. A broad toothless grin split his face as he walked over and squatted beside him next to the mooring. He nodded at the schoolbooks in his hands and spoke:

"You schoolboy, uh? You go school, uh?"

The boy surveyed the figure beside him. The sailor's face was tanned and unblemished. A single loop of gold dangled from his ear – it glinted dully in the twilight as he talked. He wore blue dungarees and a thin nondescript jacket open at the collar.

Narrow pointed boots squeezed out onto the oily pavement beneath him. Above them, the boy could feel the row of faces peering down at them. The sailor babbled:

"Yah, you schoolboy, pretty little schoolboy…"

The boy felt a sickening dread rising within him. He rose to walk away. The sailor seized his hand. Above them, the boy could feel the faces, the hungry eyes. "Nah, nah, pretty boy. You come with me. You come with sailor man."

The faces, the dark hungry eyes…

In the mist they walked through rows of serried warehouses and shanties. Here and there old men with backs bent to the rain plodded from eave to eave. Water ran in nets across the boy's face, tasting slightly of salt.

"Pull your hood up."

"I can't get any wetter."

"Pull your hood up."

He pulled his hood up. Water fled in parallel torrents on either side of them. The boy watched a dead rat roll end over end in the angry water, rushing toward the sea. Its small pink feet closed on empty air.

"I've got about twenty minutes. You still want that ice cream?"

"Yeah, sure."

He did not want ice cream. They went into a small shop, and while the boy stood near the door, the sailor went up to the counter to order.

"Give me a chocolate double-dip cone with nuts… for the kid here."

As he stood waiting, his father reached into his coat pocket and drew out a pack of cigarettes. He palmed one for a moment and jammed it into his mouth. He patted the seat of his pants with both hands and leaned over the counter.

"Hey, give me some matches with that cone, will you?"

Raw hands moved quickly inside a cardboard cylinder behind the glass. The sailor shuffled his feet and threw sidelong glances at the people beside him. The boy stood patiently by the door and watched his father's russet-colored hands clench and unclench, thinking: *Of all of us, why does he always pick me to see him off? He sees himself in me – that's why. His blood runs in all of us, but the others are not like him. They share his home but not his unrest. He will try to stop me.*

The street continued to sink toward the harbor. Thin streams of brown dripped to the pavement as the boy walked beside his father, occasionally running his tongue across the pulpy mess in his hand. The skyline presented a broken surface of gray slate roofs and towers. Through fractured houses the boy could now see ships rocking at anchor and, farther beyond, the sea itself rooted deeply between the two arms of the harbor. The drizzle had stopped, and the sun oozed like an ugly open wound on the horizon, bleeding on the water. Gulls screamed.

"Your mother says you're doing fine in school. I like to hear things like that."

"Thanks." Water filled his shoe as he walked through a puddle. He thought of the rat.

"That's the only way you're going to get out of this hellhole, you know, is through school. There are lots of people around just dying to give money away to some bright poor kid like you. You'll go far with your brains. Just keep it up."

"Thanks."

Limpid light fell on the sea city.

"Your mother says you got into a little scrape after school the other day. Something about a fight?"

"Yeah." The smell of brine filled his lungs as they came within full view of the harbor and his father's ship.

"Lick him?"

"Yeah."

"Good." The sailor tossed his cigarette butt to the ground and crushed it. "Your mother's a little skittish about stuff like that, but I think a boy should be able to take care of himself. Good."

The boy said nothing. The damp pavement gave off a faint smell of oil and fish, and a sea breeze filled his hood. From the ship came sounds of men working.

He pushed the hood from his head and spoke boldly to the sailor, his father:

"Why didn't she come with us?"

The ship reared from the ocean like an angry sea god.

"She wasn't feeling well today. You know that." A pause

followed, and then he heard his father's voice again, softly. "She's sick, you know."

The boy gazed far out over the water to the mouth of the harbor gaping like a large tongueless maw in the bleeding wash of the sun. Boats dotted the face of the bay, and a sail tacked off the distant coastline. Waves lifted and fell, capped with froth. The boy imagined facing windward and blinking at the sun resting on a landless horizon. He imagined the fellowship of the cabin, the lean whiskered faces bent over ragged cards, the decks scrubbed and sparkling in the waking sunlight, the scud flying across the surface of a blue-gray sea, and stars suspended in the jet solitude of the night watch, guides to familiar ports. A simple joy filled his spirit and ebbed as he turned – his father was gone.

In the solitude of his parents' bedroom that night, he stood concealed safely in the shadows. Earlier thoughts passed through his mind in random procession, overshadowed by thoughts of his family. He saw the faces of his brothers and sisters projected and infinitely multiplied over a boundless broken field of slate gray. In dumb phalanxes they stood, facing a faceless man wearing a sailor's uniform. In unison, the children, plastic, expressionless, lifted their arms in a gesture of supplication. With their arms still raised, the uniformed man's head began to shrivel as the children's arms fell slowly to their sides, their eyes rolling languidly in their sockets as they slumped and crumpled one by one into the embracing grayness of the field. Seawater rushed over their bodies and covered their listless faces with the color of jade and seaweed.

The boy pushed aside the sliding door of his father's closet and caressed the rough fabric of his father's uniform. He remembered the sailor's words before boarding ship, but when he drew the sleeve to his nose and once again felt the sting of salt water on his cheeks, he forgot entirely, turning his thoughts to the offing.

★ ★ ★ ★ ★

The clock pricks her awake, spitting endless trochees at the bare walls, provoking her. Guilt, embodied in an image of Susie

Quent, presents itself for several moments at the edge of her half-consciousness, and Ruth dozes and dreams fitfully, watching the images flit in and out of her torpor...

An old hag steps across the notched threshold of an old hovel made of mud and thatch. Over a shallow dish a young girl sits clad in gray tatters, pushing her spoon through the sticky lumps of cold porridge beneath her vacant eyes. Rain seeps and drops from the wattles overhead; a candle sputters near the child's elbow. The hovel is bare save for the table and two rotten logs serving as chairs – moss covers the wet rotting wood. The girl is fair-haired and smeared with soot from head to toe. Welts cover her face and shoulders, and as she eats, she mutters stray snatches of nursery rhymes in a halting singsong, occasionally looking up from her dish to watch the rain through a makeshift window punched through the thin woven wall of the hut. Sad eyes reflect the color of rain.

The hag approaches the girl and strikes her with a thick knobbed stick. The child accepts the blows in silence. As the girl's face droops toward the dish, the hag thrusts the tiny head into the porridge, croaking, "Aye, and how's that, my bonnie one? Does that suit your fancy? Gowns and phaetons for my little wench, eh?" The old woman rakes her throat, and as the girl's face rolls senselessly in the gruel she spits a glistening wad of bloodied sputum into the thin strands of gold which cover the girl's neck and shoulders. Satisfied, she draws up the other log beside the table and pulls a clay pipe out of the folds of her cloak. Smoking, she croons and cackles softly to herself. "Aye," she says. "Aye."

In a deep wood, a beautiful maiden sits on a stone beside a still green pond. It is autumn, and brilliant flecks of color dot the countryside. A bird warbles nearby. Jutting rocks float among a circle of treetops reflected in the motionless water. The girl is alone, and she sits with a dark red blossom cupped in her hand, pulling the petals off one by one and dropping them into the green pool below her. Her melancholy song passes untroubled over the face of the water:

> *On an ancient coast*
> *Stands an old turret facing seaward;*
> *The circling sea birds know its name,*
> *And sailors lost under the emerald waves.*

Resting against the brink,
A woman stands at its lofty summit
Watching breakers crash on stubbled rock,
And brine on pale wrack and bone.

In her ebbing beauty,
She looks out over the face of the deep
With ivory eyes, singing with the tempest,
And the winds lift her fading hair.

A fair young man emerges suddenly from the woods and steps to the far edge of the pool. His hair curls gracefully to his shoulders, and his strong body lies bare to the sun. The young woman looks upon his beauty and smiles, for her lover has honored their tryst.

In the choked street of a ghetto a priest walks at night through rabble and open sewers. Cars shriek and blare, casting headlights on wretched, withered faces. The priest walks on. Children cry from gutters; diseased men paw at his cassock. A prostitute leans out of a doorway and watches the clergyman approach. Green lips bend into a sneer:

"Hey, Fawduh! I hears you monk types does it wid alta' boys. How d'ya live wid ya'selves, eh, Fawduh?"

The priest stops and walks on. Behind him, the voice rasps:

"Fawduh. Hey, Fawduh!"

A gladiator strides confidently through a damp passageway and steps boldly out into the harsh light of a coliseum. Flowers rain down upon him as he crosses bleached sand to the emperor's box. Trumpets sound as the warrior lifts his arm in salute to his ruler, who signals his approbation by raising and lowering the regal scepter. His wife the empress sits beside him in the full regalia of her high station. She sits apart from all save her royal husband.

In her cold beauty, she sits apart from all.

The gladiator trains a perplexed gaze on her veiled eyes and looks down frowning as a boy approaches bearing a sword and a dagger. He grips and brandishes them defiantly at the sun and at the multitude that has come to watch him die. A thick dusty sweat covers his face and forearms as he turns to face two large gates at the distant end of the arena. He looks briefly above and behind him to see the empress touching her right ear. He smiles and crosses the hot sand in sure strides until he reaches the gates. He hesitates, then points the tip of his sword at the left door.

A lion springs out into the light as the gate rises, then stands bewildered by the sudden wave of human fury which roars forth from the throats of the spectators, by the sheer volume of human bloodlust. It growls and paws the sand, circling slowly until it sees the helpless gladiator, who crouches and begins to advance.

The struggle is brief. As the lion feeds, the empress feels its sinewy flesh against her own, its simple lust for bleeding flesh and the predator's instinct. Beside her king, apart from all, she betrays a smile.

From a thick pine forest wrapped around the base of a bald mountain an ancient woman appears, ascending steadily. She mounts the acclivity in small careful steps, following a goat path that winds its way up to the cloudy summit. The stones weep and glisten dully under a dirty, mottled sky. It is cold and damp, and the old woman's breath leaves her mouth in plumes. She stops often to rest. An eagle rises and falls far above her, gliding in and out of the muddy clouds.

A shapeless smock is draped across the woman's shoulders, and she looks straight ahead with opaque, depthless eyes. Her flesh hangs in loose folds on a slack jawbone, swaying slightly as she mutters at the blind rocks barring her way. The heavens abruptly divide and burst as a streaked gray cylinder of rain descends on the twisted, tottering figure on the side of the mountain – it strikes the craggy stone in tiny spouts and drives the woman to her knees. Rivulets appear suddenly, rushing willfully across the inert gray body, the old furrowed hands clinging desperately to the mountainside. The rain subsides, and a pale sun appears through swirling milky clouds, shining brightly on cold stone.

In the field, among tall stalks of grain, a peasant girl waits. A dry, chaff-filled breeze blows through her tangled hair, and her azure eyes mirror the sky above her.

From stalk to stalk she moves, gathering the grain with nimble hands, suddenly standing as if to hear the passing of a crow nearby or the shouting of men in the next field. She is far from home in the heart of a strange land, in the midst of goatherds and the sickle-tongued women who tend the fields beside her. Among the stalks of grain she stands, waiting for the one who will make her big with many children…

The image of Susie Quent suddenly rears like a hydra from the edge of a pristine field of white. Ruth's eyes widen and roll in horror, and the words seem equally hideous as they pierce and twist like a shaftless barb inside her heart:

"Why do you hate me, Ruth? Why? Why?"

★ ★ ★ ★ ★

"Desiderata circumscribe experience." Tommy looked up shyly, brightly. "At least I think so. Don't you?"

★ ★ ★ ★ ★

"Cliff. Clifton! C'mon, what's wrong, man?"

Her swollen cheeks returned to him, her cheeks swollen with crying.

"...and you're the only one that's ever made her cry," his little sister had bawled from the door as he entered the car with his friends. "You made her cry, Clifton!" The words had trailed behind the car like cruel rope.

"C'mon, Clifford, what's wrong?" White seized his shoulder and shook him roughly. "What the hell is wrong with you?"

Clifton stared at granite eyes, the unforgiving eyes of his sister Anne. They moved from side to side impatiently and suddenly turned to hazel, the eyes of his friend. Trevor White moved to the edge of his seat and looked beyond Clifton into the more remote areas of the bar.

"Listen, Cliff-Boy, you'd better snap out of it. We drove all the way over here to have a good time, and all you can do is sit there and mope."

Clifton followed White's eyes. In a corner, hidden in the shadows, sat a group of black girls. He turned to face his friend.

"I guess you're right. It just seemed... tougher this time, you know. I've never had that much trouble before."

"Don't you know how to handle your old lady by now? Don't let her give you any shit – put your foot down." He tapped his swizzle stick against the side of the glass. "I have no problem with mine. I kind of think she's glad to get rid of me."

"That's too bad, really, if you think about it, Trev..." Pride locked his tongue, and he stopped. The rest followed in silent fragments:

Too bad. Way too bad she can't stand the sight of her own son.

The others babbled, Tubby and Malloy. He pushed his finger through the dust on the table between them, a word written on alley walls. Tubby waved his flabby arms at him and gabbled:

"Yeah, I saw Cliffareeno at the drive-in with Jessie ... the make-out artist ... what I wouldn't do ... hear he's a real bastard when you really get to know him ha ha ... quiet one tonight though ... eat me, Malloy, you stupid sack of shit ..."

Aimed at me. My retinue minus a Falstaff.

The scene repeated itself tirelessly. He had walked quickly through the living room as if the momentum would be enough to carry him safely out the door.

"I'm going out, Mom."

She looked up from the magazine and let her glasses fall around her neck on a bright gold chain. Sensing raised voices, his little sister appeared from the next room. His mother's voice pulled him backwards:

"Oh you are, are you? Out where?"

"We're thinking about going to a movie downtown." He made a motion toward the door, not looking back. "I don't know when I'll get home."

"Now you wait just a moment, young man."

He slowed and continued.

"Clifton!"

He stopped, not turning. He felt pinned under the weight of his family's eyes, a large dead weight he had carried all his life and had only recently become aware of. His sister shuffled nearer, noisily. Behind him he could hear his mother's magazine rustling in her lap.

"You're not going out drinking again, are you, Clifton?"

He pivoted and faced her squarely. Her weak eyes and the loose flesh hanging from her narrow jaw angered him, her mole-like helplessness. He marveled at the frailness of her body in comparison to his own, the common flesh, a lion from a lamb, and his anger brimmed and gushed:

"And what are you going to do about it? What the hell can you do to stop me?"

A bright crimson colored the face of his mother as she rose and walked toward him. Her movements were rehearsed.

She's seen it coming too. I haven't given her enough credit.

He stood without moving as his mother walked within a foot of him and began to tap her finger on his chest.

"…just because I'm a woman you think you can take advantage of me if your father were here you know he wouldn't put up with this nonsense not one minute now when I say I don't want you going out that's exactly what I mean you will stay at home tonight and study it's a wonder you make the grades you do with all your fooling around…" Her finger struck his sternum in a dull bone-rhythm. She nodded toward the door. "And as for those idiot friends of yours you should be happy…"

Clifton's arms rose like two hooks and clamped his mother's limp shoulders firmly. She flinched as his hands gripped and released her bare arms, the flush receding, leaving a pinched, oily, piebald pallor.

"But he's not here, Mother – my father is not here." The heat of his anger had cooled, and a frigid bitterness tempered his voice. His tone was hushed and measured. "He finally wised up. You let him walk all over you, and when he got sick of you, he decided just to walk right on out of the house and keep walking." He leaned closer to her. "Don't you know he had a mistress? Did you really think he was 'bowling'? Why do you think he stumbled in at all hours? Why did you ignore the obvious? And why were you so *weak*? Don't you realize that about the only thing in the world he really wanted was for you to say something? That, Mother, *that* is why my father is not here to stop me."

Clifton's voice faded, and his arms fell abruptly to his sides as he watched his mother's face draw in upon itself convulsively. Her slumped back heaved; her thin hands sought and found each other like friends long parted. A thin ribbon of tears dribbled down her face toward her chin. Clifton suppressed a sudden urge to hold her and tried instead to place his hand on her shoulder again. Alarmed, she moved away and began to walk slowly out of the room. A car horn sounded outside. Proud resentment found his tongue, and Clifton responded, shouting after the pathetic retreating figure:

"I'm my father's son. I'll do whatever I want to do."

It was then that he noticed his little sister standing off to the side of him with her head slightly lowered and her feet planted squarely beneath her. She too was crying, but unlike her mother she would brook no intimidation.

Little Anne, my baby sister. The gutsiest one of the whole lot.

He stepped to the door, and she followed him with thin choking sobs. He was not surprised when her fist caught him in the small of his back. He spun around, caught her up in his arms, and pinned her to the floor. Their breath blended in shallow gasps.

"Now what the hell did you do that for? It's none of your business."

She struggled, and a stray knee dug into his back. He winced and shook her until they sat face to face, his sister's flushed and glaring. The horn sounded again. "What's wrong with you, Annie? What's gotten into you?"

She spat, and Clifton ducked as the stringy spittle arched past his head.

"I'll tell you what's wrong, Clifton!" she choked. "She never did you any harm, and all you can do is yell at her. It's just not right." She wiped her nose with the back of her hand. "You're nothing but a big bully – a big, stupid, jock bully. It's a terrible thing to see your mother cry, a terrible thing!"

Clifton rose and walked out the door. He suddenly felt stifled, and the air outside was invigorating, freer. He walked rapidly toward the jeering faces in the car. As his hand touched the door handle, his sister's voice reached him from the safety of the house:

"You're the only one that's ever made Mama cry, Clifton, the only one! Even Papa never made her cry."

The alcohol had done little to soothe him. The ride across town had been subdued by his brooding, and he sat hugging the door, staring at the passing lampposts and ignoring his friends' predictable banter. It began to rain, and he watched the water spray the mudflaps of the truck in front of them. He was not happy with himself, and his surroundings offered nothing to cheer him up. He felt for the first time in his life as if he had made an irrevocable error, an ugly blunder which he would later come to regret. It gnawed at him, and he looked out the car window like a forlorn dog. A chill touched his arm, and he swung his hips around in his seat to face its source, the intruder. It was Tubby.

"You look like you need a cold one, Cliffo. Here." The beer danced gaily in his outstretched hand. Clifton snapped out a curt "No!" and continued to scowl at the sidewalk racing monotonously past them. He could sense their rolling eyes laughing silently behind him. White's voice sliced through the car, icy and directly on target:

"Well now, boys, if the Cliff doesn't want a cold one, then I guess he doesn't want a cold one, eh? And if the Cliff wants to go ahead and stare out the window, I guess there's not a damned thing we can do about that, either. Right, boys?" The words lay flatly between Clifton and the others in the car, a challenge which Clifton left unheeded. He leaned wearily against the door and caught sight of a little boy throwing gravel at a puppy tethered to a tree in a vacant lot. As the car passed, the child stooped to embrace the cringing animal. A weak smile cramped Clifton's lips.

My friends here, my family there. Jesus H. Christ.

They had ceased talking and were whispering now, stretching their necks in the direction of the shadows. The girls were giggling, flashing their eyes and teeth at them. Clifton sensed danger as other figures moved at the periphery of the tavern. He touched White's arm.

"Let's go, White. I'm getting sick of this place."

"Oho! Clifton speaks!" White said, the others parroting him. "No, no, Clifton. Before we go, I'd like to have a little talk with these young ladies over here." He got up and swaggered crazily toward the shadows. "Maybe they're going our way." Tubby and Malloy hung their necks out over the end of the table, grinning like apes. Clifton braced himself against the back of the booth.

He's going to get himself killed, and he's taking us with him.

White teetered from side to side, and the darkness merged and separated as he caromed off table and chair on his way toward the giggles, the enticement of forbidden flesh. The shadows converged, separating him from the black girls and his friends. He stopped and stood completely still, listening intently to words too predictable to be ignored:

"What the hell you think you doin', white boy?"

Clifton nudged Tubby out of his way and walked slowly and noisily toward the circle of bent backs surrounding White. The bartender had leaned forward with his elbows on the bar, and Clifton knew immediately that he would not receive help either from him or from his own friends at the table behind him. He threw his shoulders back, trying to appear less terrified than he really was. The eyes widened as he approached, and the circle opened and closed as he stepped to White's side.

None of us belongs here, including them.

"Well now! A hero. What's your name, white boy?"

Clifton's arms felt like two thick pipes. His bowels loosened, releasing a stream of inaudible flatus.

"Clifton."

"Clifton? What the hell kind of name is that, boy?" And without waiting for an answer: "You're a big motherfucker. How come you're so motherfuckin' big, white boy?"

Clifton swallowed, trying to relax, trying to sound bold.

"I'm a football player."

"The white boy plays 'ball! Well, ain't that somethin'!" The voice suddenly shifted to White, who had rolled his shaking pale hands into fists and stuffed them into his pockets. "You! You're the asshole here. What's your name?"

White's voice was extremely shrill, and the answer came out in broken squeaks:

"Whi… Whi… White!"

"Hear that, brothers? A white boy named White!" Forced laughter followed from the dark circle. "Now that is *really* somethin'!" A slick cropped head jerked suddenly toward White and hovered in front of him. White recoiled, falling backwards into a circle of hands. Two obsidian eyes bore down on him and stared transfixed at the feeble trembling thing before them, eyes full of outrage and, to a lesser extent, pity.

"What the hell you doin' flirtin' with *our* women, *Mister* White? Where you think you're at, boy?" The face hissed and hovered. "Ain't you got enough white women back home without havin' to drive down here and bother us?" A hand swiped White's cheek playfully, and he whimpered. Clifton shifted his weight from one foot to the other.

They want him, not me. He deserves what's coming to him, and he knows it. Clifton looked from side to side. *It's him they want, not me. They'd let me go if I left right now.* A fist and knee lashed into White's torso. *He's not struggling – Trev wants them to have done with it and leave. What's holding me back? He's my friend.* Clifton could see the faces of Tubby and Malloy peering around the cheap naugahyde. *Are these his friends?* He stepped away and then back again toward the thick knot of elbows and backs. *Is Trevor White really my friend?*

A small wiry figure withdrew from the group, and a thin finger of light leaped from a closed fist. Crouching, from the balls of his feet, Clifton lunged for the dancing blade. The figure turned, squaring off to face him, and they circled each other like two clumsy bears. The knife shot toward him, and Clifton gripped the clenched fingers holding it, feeling his grasp slip and a dull keenness prick his wrist, followed by a sharp burning. The wrested knife felt wet and warm as it dropped from his fingers to the floor.

Clifton felt very heavy as he lurched after the receding form, and around him shadows began to skip and spin like elusive candle-figures reflecting his own dull fury. Through a narrow cavern Clifton flew like a dark bird of prey, driven by a woman's wailing through jagged chambers, his heart's own black threnody, the voice of his sister: *A terrible thing, Clifton. A terrible, terrible thing!* He collapsed to his knees as a victim on the altar of his own arrogant pride, thinking:

I am my father's son. I'll do whatever I want to do, sister or no sister.

And yet the sharp tips of the shoes exploding against his head and body seemed somehow comforting as darkness finally engulfed him.

★ ★ ★ ★ ★

Ruth rose shaken from her bed and busily began to towel her hair.

"Hate you? What are you talking about, Susie? I don't hate you."

Susie moved from the foot of the bed to a chair near Ruth's vanity.

"If you don't hate me, then why do you make me feel so small when I'm around you?"

"Now you're being just plain silly, Susie." She began to comb tangles out of her hair. Susie's reflection looked up at her searchingly from the mirror, and Ruth shivered, thinking of the visions which had plagued her sleep. "You're just imagining things."

"But I'm not!" Susie rose and stood behind Ruth, who edged closer to the vanity. "I just overheard Paula and Betty talking about how I spent the night with Ian McDougal last weekend – McDougal, of all people! That really didn't bother me too much until I found out that they had heard it from *you*. Now why is my own roommate going around spreading gossip about me? Tell me that."

Ruth casually shook her hair until it lay in soft serpentine coils on her shoulders. "I really don't have any idea what you're talking about, Susie." Her lips parted in a cruel smile. "'The truth will set you free,' as Amos would say."

Susie turned and walked to the window. Her arms, spread out like two delicate wings in flight, shimmered against an indigo sky. Her hands relaxed and fell from the throttled curtains; her head leaned slightly forward, her eyes following the rich lines of her figure until they rested on her bare feet. She wiggled her toes thoughtfully.

"At least I'm not ashamed of what I do. At least I can do it without hating myself for it," she mumbled to the distorted birds and trees beyond the old uneven windowpane, saying and feeling the half-truth. "At least I can admit it." A pair of squirrels bounded across a path of trampled grass.

"What did you say, dearie?" Ruth had smeared moisturizer on her legs and now sat waiting patiently for it to dry. "Are you talking to the window again?"

"No, I'm not talking to the window again! All I do is try to mind my own business, and all you can do is talk behind my back!" She shook the words out of her body. "I've never done *you* any harm."

"But it's all true, isn't it, sweet-stuff?" Ruth said serenely. "If all the things you've heard about yourself are lies, I'll take them back right now." She carefully began to remove the cream from her left ankle. "But I guess I won't have to, will I?" Her hands moved up her trim legs.

"Well, so what if they *are* true? It doesn't bother me half as much as it seems to bother you." Again, the half-lie passed unconvincingly. "It's Tommy, isn't it? Or Clifton or McDougal or Bradley or Joe or Herbert or any of the others you think I've slept with. Clifton makes you feel so cheap that you can't stand knowing another woman who doesn't let men walk all over her. You hate me because I'm free to sleep with anyone I want without depending on him, without hanging all over him like you do with Clifton. You hate me because I don't feel all used up like you." She stopped to fill her lungs. "I don't try to be some prissy two-bit slut who can't handle herself much less a relationship with any man without feeling horrible or blaming somebody else for her own problems, so if I were you, Ruth Hager, I'd take a pretty good look at yourself and the way you treat other people before I'd go on making me and yourself and everyone else in this world completely miserable with your selfish bitchiness."

Their eyes locked for a moment before Susie turned toward the window again. Behind her a soft damp pad stroked Ruth Hager's thigh in truculent hisses, and Susie sought her room-mate's image in the pane but could find none at all.

"It's because there isn't one," she said as her breath spread and faded on the glass, leaving no trace. "There's nothing to see." She touched a crossbar and traced its length down to the sill. Her own reflection looked back at her transparently. Susie touched the glass where her face appeared, outlining the eyes and mouth with her fingertips.

"As clear as ice," she whispered, and the half-lie/half-truth again emerged from the back of her mind. Her image wavered. A sharp flapping of feet sounded in the distant part of the room as Ruth crossed from the vanity to the lavatory. Susie could sense the final triumph in the voice as it spoke to her splayed back bent toward the window:

"Well, Susie, now that we've gotten that out of the way: Are you going to the party tonight?"

And after a precise interval she added:

"Tommy's taking me."

★ ★ ★ ★ ★

GENUFLECTION

Amos quickly mounted the shallow, creaking steps and turned violently to face still more flights of stairs which continued to double back and forth for the full height of the dusty building. He was exhausted and knew it, but he ascended doggedly and with great purpose. From on high came the soft patter of voices, and Amos hurried his step, but in the middle of the flight he suddenly kneeled and slapped the banister with the butt of his hand.

CONFESSION OF SIN

"I'm late, and I forgot my Bible," he said. The banister received the blow in silence.

ASSERTION OF CONTRITENESS

He shrugged and moved slowly up the remaining steps to the classroom. Inside, a small clump of students chatted. Amos, plucking a gaunt, bearded man from a group of young women, pulled him hastily to a secluded area of the room and broached the matter at hand.

"I left my Bible in my room," he said, holding his empty hands behind him.

"That's all right, Amos," the lanky man droned. He pulled at his beard and looked furtively back toward the women he had just left, who had moved closer together as if to hide something among them. "You can use mine."

"Can I? It won't happen again. I promise."

OSCVLANS ALTARIVM

"Listen, Ritter, before we begin, I have this great joke I just heard from one of my floormates." Amos' fingers crossed and recrossed behind him. "It goes like this: This bartender is in a bind, you know, and he has to find someone to take his place one evening, or else he's out of a job. He gets hold of a friend, you know, and arranges for his buddy to take over for him. 'One thing,' he says to his friend. 'This bar only caters to deaf-mutes, but they use signals to order drinks.'" Seth Ritter looked uncomfortably toward the center of the room and down at his watch. "'One finger means a beer, two a Tom Collins...'" Amos' voice trailed off as Ritter touched his shoulder.

"That's enough, Amos," he said quietly. "That's really not appropriate here."

INTROIT

Seth Ritter, student of divinity, walked away from Amos Kirk, victim of circumstances, and addressed the four corners of the room, throwing his arms out toward the young men and women in a simple gesture of gathering.

"Let's begin, people," he said. He held his thin arms out as if to embrace the air, and the students moved to both sides of him, joining hands to form a circle. The meeting was about to begin.

KYRIE ELEISON

Amos, befuddled and chapfallen, moved sheepishly to the ring of worshipers. *What have you done? What have you done?* his thoughts cried.

He bowed his head, feeling the full weight of his folly descend upon him like a thick odor, isolating him from the others around him.

GLORIA IN EXCELSIS DEO

Ritter's voice drew his thoughts out of darkness into light:
"We have much to be thankful for – the passing of winter,

the arrival of spring, the union of kindred souls here tonight. And since we live in an age of skepticism, it is a blessing to know that there exist those who have sought and found comfort and truth in our Lord Jesus Christ, and each of our meetings, in its own way, becomes a reassertion of our eternal gratitude. It is important then that we, at the beginning of each Fellowship meeting, lift our hearts in prayer to our Almighty Maker." Amos' heart tightened and expanded fitfully. "Amos, will you lead us in prayer?"

DOMINVS VOBISCVM

I have been called. It is me he has chosen. Dear Lord, Your forgiveness is indeed bountiful.

COLLECT

"Let us pray," Amos said. Around him, heads drooped obediently.

"We really do have a lot to be thankful for. Just the very fact that we're alive to experience Fellowship is enough to be thankful for. We're lucky to be living in a country where all our basic needs are provided for, and to be going to a college like Flanders where people can do as they please without fear of persecution. We're very lucky to have a Fellowship leader like Seth Ritter, who has organized and led the group for the past five years, who brought the Word to spiritually barren ground. There have been many times when I've been able to confide in him and no one else, and he's always been right there ready to help out. When I see all the ugliness around us, all the sin, it makes me proud to know somebody like Seth who really stands out from all the rest, an example for everybody. Through people like him our Christian faith is able to grow and remain strong. Oh Holy Father, on this occasion of thanksgiving, we thank You for our lives, our faith, and those special men and women who bear Your message to the ignorant. In Jesus' name we pray. Amen."

OFFERTORY

"Thanks, Amos." Heads rose; hands fell. "Now, first of all, there's a bit of business to attend to. The following people owe back dues: Fran, Bob, Pete McElroy, Pete Morris, Val, Lynn, Doug…"

ORATE, FRATRES

"It hit me on this train." A poker-faced co-ed spoke of an epiphany. "I was sitting in my compartment reading a magazine when the Spirit of God moved within me. Well, I'll tell you, I put that magazine down right away and nudged my boyfriend awake, and it's funny: he felt the same thing too. And it's been with us ever since. What's even stranger is that I was visiting my cousin out East the following spring when…"

SECRETA

Amos sat absorbed.
I sure hope those jokers don't do anything to my room while I'm gone.

SPIRITVS SANCTVS

"…believe in God and earth and Jesus Christ His Son was conceived by the Virgin Mary under Pontius was crucified dead and He descended into the third day He rose on the right hand of God to judge the quick and the dead believe in the Holy Communion of the forgiveness of the resurrection of the life everlasting amen."

Flatly, mechanically, in unison, the following intoned their faith. At a point exactly four miles above the musty classroom, a stream of air tugged plumes of clouds playfully through the sunlight.

PATER NOSTER

Sidewalks (concrete, splintered by grass and weeds, in a general state of disrepair) exist to convey humans from one point to another.

Rogues like Ian McDougal exist at particular points in time and space to make others acutely aware of their shortcomings.

McDougal the rogue paused on a splintered sidewalk and listened intently to the lyrics issuing from the window above him:

> Koom-bah-yah, my Lord,
> Koom-bah-yah.
> Koom-bah-yah, my Lord,
> Koom-bah-yah.
> Koom-bah-yah, my Lord,
> Koom-bah-yah.
> Ooooooooooooooooh Lord,
> Koom-bah-yah.

How's that go again? Bah-yah-koom? Boom-kah-yah? Sis-boom-bah?
He considered that and other problems of a less metaphysical nature, then proceeded on his way.

PAX DOMINI

Again, the ring of students formed with Seth Ritter at the center. His lean arms stretched toward them in exhortation:

"And now, in closing, I charge you to remain strong in the faith of our Father. May the peace and love of our Lord be with you all. Amen."

FRACTION OF THE HOST

Amos watched nameless knots of men and women leave a room in a decaying building; the lights dimmed and died overhead as the last student passed out of sight. Two lonely hands rested on the cracked spine of an old gaunt chair, and for a long time Amos gazed blankly at the empty door, watching a shaft of murky sunlight creep toward the barren threshold.

ECCE AGNVS DEI

O you who have held your hearts fast against the crying of forgotten children, behold the tears of Amos Kirk – the meek, the humble, the Lamb.

NON SVM DIGNVS

In an empty room, Amos offered a silent prayer:

I have erred. I have followed a path of self-righteousness, and now I am alone. I am alone now, but I shall seek Your love through others and never be lonely again. Never, never again.

He smiled, and the walls reflected the bright warmth of purpose. With a quick step, lightly, he crossed the threshold and descended the stairs, two steps at a time.

CORPVS DOMINI NOSTRI

The grass was wet, and Amos exulted in its wetness. Around him gnarled trees squatted like crouching satyrs. He touched the rough bark and looked up through matted branches at a cluster of stars.

God's gift. God's gift to share. I will befriend those I have spurned. I will love those I have hated, my brother Man.

The lights of Fowler Hall twinkled and greeted him in the distance. He ran, then slowed to a walk again.

McDougal's room. By God, I'll go visit McDougal. He won't believe it.

He stopped suddenly. Two forms appeared sitting on a park bench directly across his path.

SANGVIS DOMINI NOSTRI

He walked nearer and listened. He recognized one voice as Ritter's, the other belonging to another Fellowship member, a girl.

"Seth? Is that you?"

A head turned as Amos drew closer to the bench.

"Oh, hi, Amos. Say, I'm kind of busy talking to Val here. Don't you have some studying to do?"

"Oh, not really. It can wait." He bent toward them and drew back abruptly. The top of the girl's blouse was unbuttoned. "Hey, what are you doing to her, Seth?"

"Didn't you hear what I said, Kirk? I told you to get lost and leave us alone."

Amos did not look back. He continued ahead, directionless, permitting habit to guide him. All thoughts turned inward and shrank to the barest edge of reality, like beasts frightened by the dead thing flapping loosely in his soul.

ITE, MISSA EST.

MRS. PRENTISS:	Listen to me. He was always the quiet one, sitting around the house saying nothing to nobody. And grades? First in his graduating class, a regular genius. He was my favorite of the bunch, the one I had the highest hopes for. But quiet. Kids would stop by once in a while, but he refused to see them, not pouting or anything, just sitting off by himself. And then that night, after his graduation, the whole family together for once in the dining room, he says he's joined the navy. Scholarships running out of his ears, and he joins the navy!
PHOEBE PRENTISS:	We was talking about Stevie.
PENDORO:	You butcher our mother tongue, child.
MCDOUGAL:	Listen, it doesn't make any difference. What I can't believe is how the dumbshit brought it up right in the middle of the meal.
MR. PENDORO:	Well, well. The boy's finally made it. Flanders a fine institution, a good education blah blah…
MCDOUGAL:	Thomas Pendoro II, C.P.A.
PENDORO:	Sons follow fathers, and fathers follow fathers.
FIRST MATE ROLLINS:	Prentiss, eh? John's boy? Well, since you're a grown man and all, I see no harm in telling you a story about your father when we were with the merchant fleet. He sure was a crazy son of a bitch…

MRS. PRENTISS:	You could've heard a pin drop, it was so quiet. John leaned across the table and collared him and began to shake him till his teeth rattled. I hated to see it in front of the children, you know, Stevie being the oldest and looked up to and all. I started to scream, but John threw his hand at me like he does sometimes so I shut up. And in front of the little ones! I hated to see it in front of the children.
PHOEBE PRENTISS:	Red as a beet, big veins sticking out all over his head, yelling like crazy at Stevie.
HAGER:	Graduation? It was grand. Trala-lala-la. Dancing all night. Like prom.
JOHN PRENTISS:	My son, my son.
KIRK:	His Son. My Savior, oh Jesus.
HAGER:	And Daddy with my shiny new cabriolet. Oooooh! It was fantastic.
PRENTISS:	I told him, but he wouldn't listen. He never listened because he was never there to listen.
KIRK:	You knew what would happen.
PENDORO:	Beware of pederasty, Stefan.
MCDOUGAL:	And Turks wearing gold.
PENDORO:	One expects nothing less from our elders: we become what we are.
MCDOUGAL:	Enough. Speak of infidelity, woman.
MRS. FLAXTON:	I regret nothing. He was always gone, always at the office. I raised his child. That was my only obligation.
KIRK:	But your son, ma'am – he surely must have known.

QUENT:	We all know.
PENDORO:	First-person plural, simple-present active indicative (superfluous modifier).
HAGER:	Of course *she* would know…
JAMIE PRENTISS:	So he stood up and started to cry and Dad waved his arms and…
PRENTISS:	…and I left, and it did my heart good. It did my heart good to be rid of the whole lot of them.
HAGER:	Dad and Mom and Buffy all waving from the driveway. I'd packed alone that morning and met Mom on the way downstairs. "You're a big girl now," she said. "Don't let me down. Remember everything I've told you."
CLIFTON:	Which was?
MCDOUGAL:	Enumerate, tyro.
PENDORO:	1) "Avoid sleeping with your professors." 2) "Be discriminating about your sexual partners." 3) "In general, try to show better judgment than you did in high school." 4) "Be a good girl" (said *en passant* to lend levity to the pervasively monitory tone of the conversation).
MCDOUGAL:	More matter with less art, Pendoro. Speak English or shut up for once in your life.
ARENSON:	You can strike item one in your case, Tommy.
A SAILOR:	He seemed straight to me. But then I was passing by a bulkhead one night and holy Jesus…

A TEACHER:	I cornered him once and asked him whether he was interested in the material or the grade. And do you know what he said?
PENDORO:	No. What did I say?
A TEACHER:	He said, "Neither, sir. Your class provides an opportunity to measure the extent of my ingenuity, for I have yet to crack a text-book." Precocious, and very obnoxious about it.
A COUNSELOR:	Let's talk long-term, Tommy. Flanders grads get jobs. That's all there is to it.
MR. PENDORO:	Exshellent choish, Flandersh ish. Shimply exshellent.
PENDORO:	Let's talk education for education's sake, gentlemen. Let's talk of means rather than ends.
MCDOUGAL:	Some people never leave school. Why put things off? Live, buy, consume, die.
A GRANDFATHER:	He was so shy he couldn't face them, apparently. Left his lunch money up on the windowsill and ate crayons instead, staring out at the empty playground. He should never have gone to one of those public schools, anyway. That's where they first begin to stray.
KIRK:	Suffer little children…
A GRANDFATHER:	He was standing outside when I came to pick him up, his teacher right beside him. Said he refused to leave school. I pulled him away from her and asked him why he didn't want to go home.

A TEACHER:	He was crying when I found him in a closet behind a bunch of old coats, and he had been crying ever since I had called his guardian. The old coot showed up an hour later demanding to know what we had done to his little Amos. When he saw the child, he pulled him away from me. "What is the meaning of this, young man?" he yelled at him. "Why didn't you get on the bus with the other children?" And Amos, as little as he was, looked up at the old man, crying so hard he could hardly breathe, and said, "They're not scared of nothing here. They're not scared of you, not scared of Jesus. Nothing, Grandpa, nothing." I'll never forget that look he gave me as he walked out of sight, as if I had betrayed him.
PENDORO:	Filiopiety is not reflexive, nor is it symmetric. Filiopiety is ideally transitive.
A GARDENER:	I'd been working for them for well onto twelve years. I was minding my own business, just like I always do, not asking for any trouble, trimming a hedge and getting to the point in the afternoon when I always start thinking about dinner, when I looked over the hedge and saw Miss Ruth lying there sunbathing in the nude. Completely naked, with her eyes closed. Of course I could do nothing but stare, Miss Ruth being a real beauty. By God, it made me feel young again. Well, some folks say that if you stare at people long enough, they'll finally figure out you're staring at them, and sure enough, she finally opened her eyes and looked at me like she knew I was there all

along. I didn't know what to do, and in fact I was getting ready to apologize when she wagged her finger at me and grinned. "Come here," she said.

CORNELIUS HAGER: Mr. Axletree, you have just been released from your contract.

PENDORO: Or, dysphemistically speaking, canned, fired, squelched, snuffed, trampled, crushed, and so on. A whipping boy. A chump.

McDOUGAL:
Jailbait Ruthie,
Jailbait Ruthie,
Seductress supreme
With a smile full and toothy.

A GARDENER: But God, boys, it was worth it, job or no job. Made me feel young again.

CLIFTON: My body is my temple. I shall want no other.

A CO-ED: Hi.

A PREDATOR: Listen, baby, you're bright, even likeable, but you're dumpy and unattractive. No guy in his right mind is going to take a second look at you. If I pay some attention to you, will you let me look at your classnotes and then disappear when the semester is over? It's all really very simple.

CLIFTON: Relieved of all inhibitions and social restraints, the male animal would fuck indiscriminately. There's no way off the Wheel.

A BODHISATTVA: Live between the Cause and the Effect.

QUENT/PENDORO: Juxtapose the terms "misogynist" and "misanthrope" meaning, respectively, a hater of women and a hater of humankind.

	A discrepancy immediately and inexcusably obtrudes itself into the mind of the more sensitive humanist: no counterpart to the former term exists in the English language. Where the female gender and the generic concept are represented, the male designation is altogether lacking. This is a travesty of the unisexualism that purportedly characterizes our age.
HAGER/CLIFTON:	Reflection excites the conscience. Don't "re-" anything. The world is fine as it is. Exist, don't think.
PENDORO/HAGER:	(?).
CLIFTON/QUENT:	(?).
PENDORO:	Yes, I remember. It was after my three high-school buddies Martin, O'Neal, and Donovan died in a head-on collision out on Highway 27. The funeral was like any other, really – it's what happened afterwards that sticks in my mind. We were standing out in the parking lot waiting to see who would be the first to leave. I didn't know very many of them – those guys had had a lot of friends. Suddenly we were all holding each other in one big group, all of us supporting each other, some people I didn't know and some people I really didn't even care for. I thought: *There is hope. There must be hope.*
ALL:	Alive, alive oh…
MCDOUGAL:	"A pessimist is nothing more than an embittered optimist."

– Thomas Pendoro

A platitude, Pendoro. Tell us something new for a change.

PRENTISS: Spartan life – self-denial – singleness of purpose. Ideals we hold near and dear.

CLIFTON: But where do you come from? Who are your parents? And what do they do for a living?

A SAILOR: I tried to keep it hushed up, but it was impossible. Everybody knew about it. They discharged them both when we got back to port. It's almost like they wanted to get caught. Jesus, it turns my stomach just to talk about it.

MRS. QUENT: They grow up so fast. They're almost uncontrollable. Her father knew nothing about Joel. I knew what she had done, but I let it go. That's the only way they learn.

MR. QUENT: I neglected her. I admit it. I tried to do things with her, but I really couldn't get my heart into it. Ever since her brother died it was really never the same again. She could tell, too, but I'll be damned if I could do anything about it. Maybe there's still time.

McDOUGAL: A bitch in heat. Thought she was going to knock me down trying to get into the sack with me. "Fine, fine," I said. A wild-ass too. But when it was all over and done with, she gave me the old Pendoro treat-ment, staring at the ceiling and not saying a word. I need her around like I need a hole in the head.

COACH RODGERS: Prentiss, I need to speak with you in private.

KIRK: Let this bitter cup pass by me.

A GRANDMOTHER: There will come a time, Amos, when…

HAGER:	Hello, Rachel? I'm just calling to tell you that I won't be able to go out to the lake this weekend. Daddy has to go to Colorado on another business trip or something, so Mom and I are tagging along to kill some time. What? Mostly shopping, I guess, although some friends of ours are going to have some kind of party up at their cabin. I think we're going to spend a few days after that in Vegas, so I guess I won't see you until we get back. Have fun at the lake! Bye-bye.
PENDORO:	It's interesting to note how we'll overlook the most blatant foibles in a person of the opposite sex only to satisfy our most basic desires.
McDOUGAL:	That is, every wench has a vaginal wrench with no reversing ratchet.
DEAN FLAXTON:	Our institution, financially straitened as it is, attempts to attract only the brightest of students.
MR. PENDORO:	They thought that I hadn't fully assessed the extent of the problem. Sure, I knew it was a problem. A drink here, a drink there – it adds up after a while. I'm no fool. I knew what was going on even when she walked out on me, but I feel and have always felt that a man is entitled to at least one shortcoming, one vice, one heroic flaw. After all, who brought home the bacon all those years? Who was the provider? So when she walked out, I really didn't care. I'd seen it coming. To hell with her, I say.
KIRK:	Pills?

MR. PENDORO: And that son of mine, the so-called "intellectual". I can't tell you how many nights I walked in to find him with his nose in some goddamned book. No balls. No hormones. A eunuch.

PENDORO: I cannot and will never equal or surpass the fancied achievements of my father.

MR. PENDORO: "Why don't you go out and do something crazy like the other kids your age?" I'd say to him. "Have I raised some kind of queer? Where's your sex drive?" When I was his age…

PENDORO: Manumit me. Liberate us from your silly prejudices, Father. Free my generation.

PROFESSOR BONSON: Try to imagine teaching the same course material semester after semester. Imagine student apathy, stacks of poorly written papers and essays, long hours, poor pay, low demand in a flooded field, tests, lectures, convocations, seminars, symposia, conferences, councils, and committees. All of that combined with the ever-present fear of tenure denial. Imagine that.

JANITOR NEWELL: You'd think they could at least make it to the bathroom. God, what a mess.

QUENT: Men.

PENDORO: But they know. Women stand apart and deride us, our wars and machinations. They intue everything.

MCDOUGAL: Media saturation
\+ Parental pressure
\+ Peer pressure
\+ Internal pressure
\+ Repression
\+ Confused ideals

What's the sum, my friends?

KIRK:	I walk to the door. I enter. I laugh. I cross to the overturned bed and sit.
HAGER:	I heard. I heard not.
PENDORO:	I saw.
McDOUGAL:	I foresaw.
PRENTISS:	I wasn't there.
QUENT:	It was horrible.
MUNRO:	Listen, Prentiss, you'll never make it to med school at this rate.
FINCH:	You light it. I'll run.
A MAGYAR CRONE:	I see a long voyage in front of you, young man. You will pass through many lands before you finally reach your journey's end.
McDOUGAL:	Yet the sailor decamped with dignity. This too I foresaw.
PENDORO:	There are as many perceptions of a man as there are men to perceive him, perceptions which, when taken together, swell and recede in endless negation like waves in a harbor. Wherein lies the man?
THE CRONE'S SISTER:	Sadness too will be yours, and scorn. Tread the way carefully, my son. Do not bruise your feet.
McDOUGAL:	I have no past. I have no ties to bind me. I was an orphan, and now I am a hyena. Ask anyone who doesn't know me.
PENDORO:	Self-fulfillment first, and recognition secondarily. The poetry is my own, to consecrate or desecrate as I please. I write for myself.

A STUDENT:	In brief:

1) Shower, shave, shit
2) Go to classes (maybe)
3) Eat
4) Go to classes (maybe)
5) Screw around
6) Eat
7) Study (maybe)
8) Screw around
9) Sleep

You'd be amazed at how little I have to study here. I was.

HAGER:	Castles in the air…
PENDORO:	…and the most difficult thing to confront on reaching adulthood is the unsoftened truth that all the garbage they feed us when we're young, viz. Robin Hood, Babe Ruth, Abraham Lincoln, Roland, William Tell, Beowulf, Cinderella, Pinocchio, Washington's cherry tree, Andrew Carnegie, Henry Ford, Snow White, Florence Nightingale, Lochinvar, Asgard, Olympus, Camelot, Achilles, Odysseus, and a host of others is just so much horseshit. Just so many shattered myths.
QUENT:	Not shattered, Tommy. Changed. I felt it too.
McDOUGAL:	Myths? What myths?
RITTER:	Believe. I too once strayed from the flock. The tug of the flesh tainted me, but now I am pure to sing out in jubilation. Hallelujah!
QUENT:	The flesh is willing, and the spirit is weak.
KIRK:	…thinking: *What now? What should I do now?*
A GRANDMOTHER:	A nice, quiet boy. It came as quite a shock.

MCDOUGAL:	Sitting at the next table with his plump wife, sitting there with his nose in a plate of meat and potatoes, grinning from ear to ear as if to say, "Hey, I'm Mr. Lower-Middle-Class, yet here's my daughter at a top college. I'm really hot shit." I'll bet his friends get sick to death of hearing about it all the time. God, it made me feel like putting a hand on his fat shoulder as if to say, "Hi, I'm Ian McDougal. I screwed your nice daughter a couple of days ago, and she sleeps with just about anything with three legs." That would have taken him down a notch or two.
ROLFE:	Jo-Jo, I got a buck here that says you can't hit McDougal over there in the head with this banana. One whole dollar.
KIRK:	Ouch!
A PLAYMATE:	'Sblood!
KIRK:	Yeth. Nanna come she make pain better say Jeezle make all better too. Jeezle make hurt go away.
A FOSTER-HOME SUPERVISOR:	I was indeed impressed. Their credentials, references…everything was in order. Of course, there is a certain probationary period – we can't very well give children away to anyone who walks in here. I was impressed the very first time I met them. A bright, happy couple, well on in years but financially secure and more than capable of raising the child. The child itself was very shy, and I felt that at last I had found a suitable couple for it. God knows the child deserved the best after all it had been through – unwed mother, vagrant father, unwanted child. You know the rest.

KIRK:	*Dear Grandmother and Grandfather...*
MCDOUGAL:	"Sanctimony," Pendoro called it. "Religious *hauteur.*" He's right, but I still wish he'd shut up sometimes.
HAGER:	Dead? *(That's really...)* Dead? *(Who again?)* Dead? *(That's really going to...)* Dead? *(Who again?)* Dead? *(That's really going to mess up my...)* Dead? *(Who again?)* Dead? *(Who?)* He's dead?
	You know, that's really going to mess up my plans for the weekend.
DEAN FLAXTON:	Contact the next of kin, send the effects home hush hush.
PENDORO:	In another avatar, amigo. The rest of us live for moments.
CLIFTON:	I found it one day when I went into his room to borrow his dictionary. He'd been writing something the night before when I'd walked by. I found it scribbled on the back of a campus bulletin. I bumped into him later that afternoon in the hall and told him I had seen the poem. I told him I liked it. When I asked him if I could look it over again, he walked away and jerked his thumb toward his room. "Check my roomie's ashtray," he said. I'm sure he was kidding, but I swear to God there are times when I really can't figure that guy out.
MRS. PENDORO:	You'd think that after eighteen years of taking care of him he'd feel some sort of gratitude. You'd think he'd want to go out and make something out of himself instead of living like some kind of Bohemian. No, it didn't surprise me – he was good at cutting classes in high school too. He's a bum. A bum.

MCDOUGAL: That night Pendoro came back late. Said he'd been at Frank's drinking with a Methuselah, a bodhisattva. He threw the garbage can down the steps again and then went to his room to throw some furniture around in there until the resident advisor showed up and told him to knock it off. One crazy bastard.

PENDORO: Down, down, down it descended in crashing thumps to the landing below me; madly swirled the twirling furniture in vertiginous pirouettes across the curling tile. The pundit had revealed the depthlessness of his sagacity.

And I was so fucking stoned.

STROMBERG: Reality is for those who can't face up to drugs.

MCDOUGAL: He has a sense of humor, at least. I talked Cliff into renting a chain saw from a hardware store across town. At five the next morning we were up with all the windows open and our headgear on, sawing away at the old dresser Cliff had been trying to get the college to fix for weeks. Hager was there smoking a cigarette, and we had the whole floor outside our door trying to figure out what was going on. And I thought Pendoro was going to laugh himself sick.

PENDORO: The Humor Continuum can be diagrammed as follows:

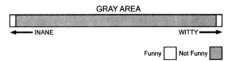

125

Some things are terribly witty, while some are terribly inane – both can be amusing. An example: My uncle opened up a delicatessen in the Holy Land called Cheeses of Nazareth. This egregious pun falls somewhere in the middle of the Continuum, bearing right.

For the most part, things are hopelessly gray, even the concept of a Humor Continuum.

MCDOUGAL: That's offal.

STIPPS: Bill is with Sue is with Tom is with Katie is with Joe is with Liz is with Hank is with Beth is with Trent is with Ellen is with Ira is with Nancy is with Logan is with Tina is with Paul is with Nicole is with Bobby is with Julie is with Ken is with Lisa is with Doug is with Mary is with Larry is with Beatrice is with John is with Jane is with Fred is with Gwen is with Rob is with me. Or haven't you heard?

HAGER: Depilate my conscience.

A BUREAUCRAT: And I repeat: There was absolutely no pressure on him to leave this institution. There was a potential scandal, yes, but no pressure whatsoever.

PRENTISS: But...

A BOOSTER: Best running back that ever came out of this town. There's no one who could even touch him nowadays. Took the wife to the game a few years ago to see him play: ham sandwiches, tuna salad, beer, quite a spread. A real scorcher, though, but it was worth it. Saw him score three

	touchdowns. The kid came out of nowhere and became a state champion. The scouts were really after him, but he opted for the navy for some reason.
A TREE:	Their eyes bend boughs.
A PEDAGOGUE:	If you would direct your attention to the following, please…
AN EMBITTERED OPTIMIST:	With puberty comes Atlas' burden. I know what it was to ride trikes and put gum in girls' hair. I have read the words of the ancients without invoking tawdry symbolism. I have been young.
QUENT:	To love, to shun…
CLIFTON:	I got tired of her after a while. You get tired of anyone after a while. The steady thing was kind of nice in a way, but in the end I had to dump her for my own good. She was taking up way too much of my time.
PENDORO:	Love doesn't have to convince us of anything.
CLIFTON:	A damned nuisance after a while, really. It's not good to keep a relationship going that long. Greener pastures, and all that.
McDOUGAL:	Love is a many-veinèd thing.
HAGER:	Fala-lala-la. Jock for poet, athlete for artist. It'll be different, better. Fala-la.
PENDORO:	You could call infatuation a distorted sense of perception. It's like walking out into a beautiful lake and realizing when you're halfway out that you're only ankle-deep. And you suddenly realize that it's not a lake you're standing in, but a mire.

KIRK: *When you get this, you won't understand but I understood when I did it, and even though I've committed my soul into the hands of your Devil I know now that I have little else to say but that I saw the hands of the Hypocrite on the flesh of the Apple, and after that there is nothing left to believe in. The pillars of your temple collapsed and the temple you built turned out to be weaker than either you or I ever suspected. People either are or aren't sinners, I can't tell any longer, and I really don't know why it's so important whether they are or aren't, so what next? All of this really scares me. It really does.*

McDOUGAL: I foresaw, but I held my tongue. They don't like prophets around here.

III

So there I was, sitting in this sweltering classroom and watching the second hand on the clock on the front wall go around and around. Don't ask me what the fool up front was talking about – I couldn't tell you. I used to pass the time by checking out the chicks sitting around me, but I can't do that anymore since I have to sit in back. All I can see now are puffy asses and cellulite. Fine. So I started to draw pictures in class – you know, birds, trees, people I know, other stuff. But now and then the t.a. would drop a question in my lap to make me look like a real ass. He hates me because I never pay any attention in class and ace all his exams. Suits me fine, it really does, but I hate being made a fool of, so I dropped the drawing. So there's little else to do now but sit around and look stupid. "God save us from fools and teachers," Pendoro says, teachers' fool. "God save me from Pendoro" is what I say.

I was thirsty too and getting thirstier by the minute thinking about a tall cool one resting in the palm of my hand. I went out drinking with Cliff the other night and listened to him bitch and moan about Hager for a couple of hours. He just couldn't stop talking about her. "Glad to be rid of her," "load off my back," and on and on. I know drinking and feeling sorry for yourself go hand in hand, but I shouldn't have to sit and listen to some guy bellyache about some worthless bitch for hours on end. "What's Pendoro have that I don't have, Mac?" he kept asking me.

Boy, he had me there. Pendoro's all right in his own way, I suppose, but when you stick him beside an obvious stud like the Cliff, I see no comparison, knowing Hager's type. What gets me about the whole thing is that he was really hung up on her, Mr. "Lady's Man" Clifton himself. Sure, he'd deny it if you asked him about it point-blank, but it's easy to see by the way he keeps going on and on that he's nuts about her. I tried to change the subject, but when he got to talking about Susie, I clammed up. There's little to say there.

They're smart, though. They design these chairs so they cut right into the middle of your back so you can't doze off. I used to sit up front with all the brownnosers so I wouldn't fall asleep. It worked out all right until we started having those all-night poker games in Rolfe's room. Fell asleep one day about five feet in front of the lectern. From then on I went straight to the last row of chairs with no questions asked. If I can't hear the lecture, so much the better.

I'm being sent to this school to stare at trees. If anyone in the administration had any brains, they'd call off classes on a hot day like this. They stick us in ovens and expect us to learn something. I'll tell you what really helps me get through it all is this beanpole who sits right beside me. All he does is sit there with his god-damned finger up his nose all hour long "cleaning out the dance hall", as they say. He doesn't mess around, either. He does it with relish, with abandon. By God, there are times I think he's trying to get his whole arm up there, picking and scraping and waving his neck around like a big giraffe. It's truly a sight to see. The others try to ignore him, but I don't because there's nothing else to look at back here except crumbling plaster and the backs of people's heads.

You'd think with all the money this college is supposed to have they'd put some of it into maintenance. But no, no. You can bet your bottom dollar that most of it's probably lining some fat old trustee's pocket right now for his stable of Mercedes and his high-class whores. This place has prestige, sure, but it's not going to have it much longer if one of the rusty fire escapes collapses or one of the old ramshackle dorms goes up in smoke with eighty or so students inside. No wonder enrollment is falling off. Hell, I wouldn't have come here myself if I'd had my head screwed on straight.

But the bars, the bars. If I couldn't go down for a beer every afternoon, I'd go ahead and slit my throat just to get it all over with. I already had the scene set up in my mind: the door, the cheap carpet, the stool. "Yeah, fill 'er up, Biffer," I'd say. "Give me some head on that one, or just give me some head, period," I'd say, just to make him smile, ease his afternoon a little bit. I always like to sit there watching the guys wander in in twos and threes and maybe poke some old codger in the ribs in the meantime, just to hear what he has to say.

But no, there I was instead, sitting in some stuffy classroom surrounded by chimps and eggheads. Things were getting so bad that I was actually listening to the guy babbling up front when the bell finally rang. Did I clear out of there fast? What a stupid question.

The Sow's Ear Saloon is about a ten-minute walk from campus. I used to go to Florin's until they got so many fruits in there that you couldn't walk in without getting your ass pinched or sit down without wondering *who* was sitting next to you, if you know what I mean. Me, I'm satisfied with the bare essentials. I don't need some goddamned crystal ball spinning around in the middle of the room or foot-thick shag or groovy guys and groovy chicks strutting around in skintight designer jeans. I'd just as soon go somewhere where you can relax without feeling any pressure to get laid. Some places are completely geared for that, you know. Drinking with the boys is one thing; fooling around with women is another. They just don't mix.

So I had my sights set on the Sow, walking along as I was telling you, when this little urchin walks up to me mumbling something with this dumb look on his face like he's up to no good, and sure enough, he spits out a mouthful of sunflower seeds at me, shells and everything. Never seen the little brat before in my life, and he walks up and does that to a complete stranger. I felt like wringing his little neck, but he scampered off before I got a chance to lay a hand on him. What are they teaching them these days?

I remember that when I was a kid I used to sit beside this big ugly guy in the refectory who used to slobber all over himself like a pig. Not only that, but his nose ran like twin rivers. A real loser, let me tell you. So one day he decides he wants an extra piece of bread or something else so, fat greedy slob that he is, he walks back to the kitchen to bum one off a cook he played kiss-ass with – you know, a little extra pudding here, an extra piece of cake there. You know the kind. So while he's gone, I go for the old gum-in-the-stew routine while telling everybody watching to clam up or else. Spudgrubber returns with that extra slice of bread tucked away neatly in his gut somewhere and little crumbs of contentment stuck to the corners of his mouth. He sits down –

barely slapping his pudgy ass down on the bench before shoveling a forkful of stew into his ugly puss – and starts bolting and wolfing like he hasn't seen a morsel for days.

Well, I sat watching him out of the corner of my eye, watching that fork (it was a blur) work its way toward the gum. When it left his plate, you can bet I acted real interested in my own meal, especially when all the slurping and snorting and chomping stopped all of a sudden. Did he look around? Did he say, "Who's the big wise guy?" No. All he did was slap me in the head so hard I couldn't see straight for three days. McDougal's luck, that's what I call it – the story of my life.

I spied Joe Finch walking across the street, and I crossed to join him, nearly losing my life in the attempt, goddamned Sunday driver.

"Where are you off to, Joe?" I asked, knowing better.

"The Crusades, where do you think?" he said. Master of the one-liner, Joe Finch. "Where else would I be going on a hot Friday afternoon?" He gave me the once-over. "I'd guess you're going to the same place I'm going, McDougal, if I know you at all." How true, how true. Joe's a good sort: big Missouri boy, corn-fed, stocky, good-natured. I can actually stand him.

"Yeah, yeah," I said. "I just sat through Bonson's calculus class. He had his t.a. in there again. Boring as hell."

"A cold one will set things right, McDougal." He sure hit it on the head with that remark, *right* on the fucking head.

Finch got me to thinking about teaching in college and about how they all think they own the world and how they're all such incredible megalomaniacs (as You-Know-Who would say, popping off with his worthless ten-dollar ear-pleasers). God, it makes me ill, it really does. And Bonson likes to send in this guy in his mid-twenties to teach a bunch of pimply kids in their late teens. Can they send in an honest-to-God professor every day after we've shelled out our life's savings for a decent education? No, he has to send in some rookie teaching assistant with a thick Rumanian accent who has his head so high up in the clouds that he can't even explain a simple algorithm.

Bonson's not much better himself. I went to him once with a problem just to see if he could deal with students better one-on-

one. I swear to God, it took him half an hour to explain it to me, blabbing on about this and that and drawing from about eight different branches of mathematics and finally getting so flustered that he had to send me back to the Rumanian. Completely incompetent as a teacher. I kept smiling while I watched him since I couldn't stop thinking about Prentiss catching him at the whorehouse. His head can't be completely in the clouds, at least not his small one, if you know what I mean.

Bonson's rambling reminds me of Pendoro. Pendoro will get himself so wrapped up in what he's saying after a while that even *he* doesn't know what he's talking about. He lectures, just like Bonson. Now I like Pendoro fine, don't get me wrong, but Jesus Christ he's hard to talk to.

Like the day before, for instance. I'm in my room alone when Pendoro appears out of nowhere and walks right in. He sits down in my recliner and reaches into my bag of Coconut Cream Delights and asks me what's going on. Nothing, I say. I guess he thought that that was an invitation to shoot his mouth off for a solid hour because that's exactly what he did, sitting there going on and on about (get this) the "universality of man", meanwhile stuffing my gourmet cookies into his mouth. You can imagine me propping my eyes open while listening to stuff like "the essential man is virtually ubiquitous" and "race delineates but can never separate". I couldn't stand that for very long, so I turned the conversation to poetry since I knew that that's one thing he wouldn't have much to say about, and sure enough, he just sat there with his mouth full of cookies, wordless.

I told him poets were latter-day gloryseekers – you know, the whole Achilles shtick – and told him if he had any brains he'd drop the "campus poet/philosopher" bullshit and go money-grubbing like the rest of us. He said something about burning his poetry, and I said he wasn't sure of himself yet, so he burned his stuff so nobody could knock him off his high horse. Prentiss has gotten a look at a few of his poems and said they suck, but I really wouldn't take *his* word for anything, if you know what I mean. One thing's for sure, though – Pendoro has the whole women's floor sapped into thinking he's Milton incarnate or something like that thanks to Hager, who happens to be in love with the jerk. Women can be so gullible sometimes.

Well, off he goes like a shot into his room, and I think I'm finally rid of the guy, only he comes back with a scrappy piece of paper in his hand and lays it in my lap, telling me to read it. *Jesus Christ*, I say to myself. *I don't want to read some stupid poem right now.* So I tell him I've got some work to do and I'll read it later, which finally gets him out of the room mumbling something about thanks for the cookies, the lousy bastard. I stuck the poem in my pocket and forgot about it.

By this time, I was getting pretty sick of threading my way through the downtown mob and listening to Finch yak about this redhead he's been giving it to. It really amazes me how many people there are in this town, and I guess there must be some kind of alarm somewhere that drives them all downtown on Friday afternoon thick as thieves. Christ. There I am, trying to listen to Finch and having to dodge all these kids and dogs and bikes and middle-aged women and all the time thinking about those special one-dollar draws they have down at the Sow during happy hour. I see this poodly-looking woman coming out of this fancy boutique in front of us with a stack of boxes about five feet over her head and she's gabbing away at some spindly old blonde next to her and Finch is talking to me and the next thing you know I'm picking boxes off the pavement with Finch trying to apologize to the old bitch and with her not listening at all, just yap-yap-yapping about lawyers and husbands, and I'm almost at the breaking point, thinking: *Lady, step into my shoes for a second, just for one second.*

When we finally got her going on her way, I see the sign of the Sow poking out into the street like an oasis, and Finch says, "How would you like to be married to *her*, McDougal?" and only half-way hearing what he's saying, I say, "Yeah, sure, Jo-Jo," and down we go, the Sow's Ear being in the basement of an old hotel.

And who should greet us from the bar but the old Ear himself, George Shapiro Finestein. A mouthful, eh? Well, you can guess by the "-stein" tacked onto the end of his name how big his nose is, but Georgie's all right, believe me. Many's the time he's set me up with drinks on the house just to keep my tongue flapping, and that's fine by me. A good one, George is. And we'd just stepped in off the street when he yelled at me from the bar:

"Well, Macko! How's the Bachelor of Farts?"

Sure, it got my eyes rolling, but you have to ignore these things sometimes.

"Can't complain," I said. "Say, you know Joe Finch, don't you, Georgie?" A handshake, the usual bullshit. We sat down.

"A hot one today, huh?" Georgie opened with. "Drove the wife down to the hair parlor and had to double-park until some tinhorn threatened to ticket me, which meant that I had to drive in circles for half an hour sweating like a whore in church and waiting for her to come out, with every guy and his dog jammed up downtown in heavy traffic. But this is the killer: I'm sitting in my convertible baking, waiting for a parking space to open up somewhere when by God one opens up about a block away from the parlor. I stick the coin in the meter and turn around to see Dora walking towards me bitching about how the heat had ruined her hairdo. And I'll be damned if her hair looked any different than before. What a day."

I agreed with him and thought about how you could do just about anything to Dora – dress her up nice, get her a fancy hairdo – and she'd still be as dumpy and ugly as ever. Don't get me wrong: Dora's the salt of the earth (she comes down and helps Georgie out even though she's holding down another job of her own), but she looks like someone has been beating her with an ugly-stick since the day she was born. No shit.

Georgie was right about one thing, though – it was hotter than hell outside. I was still sweating, in fact, and Finestein was going on about doodly without noticing that me and Finch were sitting there beerless.

"Just between you and me, McDougal, I occasionally go down to this strip joint a couple of blocks from where me and the wife live for a couple of pops and of course to check out the girls. It's a circuit, you know – new strippers every week. It gets the blood pumping, and even though Dora would kill me if she knew, I figure what she doesn't know won't hurt her. She always wonders why I come home at night sometimes hornier than a dog. It's those goddamned rug dances – they get me every time…"

I finally waved two fingers at Biffer, who was sitting down at the other end of the bar.

"Hey, sorry, Mac," Georgie said, looking real apologetic all of a sudden. "Sure, sure," I said. Stupid moron.

"Well, anyway," he went on, "that night I sneaked out of the house early to catch both shows. I was feeling pretty good. It was a week ago, and I always like to unwind at the end of a work-week, you know. I sat down and ordered the usual, waiting for the show to begin when out comes this guy in a G-string, shaking his ass all over the place. 'Where are the girls?' I shouted. 'I didn't come in here to watch…'"

Prentiss. I thought of Prentiss then. I think I heard it from Liz Canfield first, although Pendoro filled me in on the details later on. What a story. Always saying he was going out looking for pussy when all the time he was probably heading down to Florin's or Georgie's gay bar for an eyeful of cock. Not to mention his buddy Rodgers. What a stud he turned out to be.

I kind of half-listened to Finestein ramble on for a while, checking out the ball game on the radio and occasionally putting in my "Yeahs" and "Sures" just to keep him happy. The Peach City Bluejays were playing Strawville, and it took me back to the days in the orphanage when I'd lie there in the dorm listening to all the snoring and wheezing with one ear and to the ball game with the other. I kept a radio and an earplug that I'd stolen from a department store hidden under my pillow, and when the lights went out, the radio went on. (There were times when that radio was about my only friend, I guess.) I always rooted for Peach City because one of the nuns told me once that my mother came from there. I'd listen to their games night after night, lying there scared to death that someone was going to snatch that radio from me and ask me where it had come from.

I guess I really don't need to tell you what happened next: Spike McClanahan was up with the bases loaded, two outs in the bottom of the ninth, tied ball game, when suddenly ZIPPP! Out came the earplug. Next thing you know, I'm standing in Mother Superior's chamber in my pajamas, rubbing my eyes and making up lies about the radio and knowing that it wasn't going to do any good since we all know that nuns are trained mindreaders. I remember it took them about ten minutes to make me feel so goddamned guilty that I would have crawled back to that department store on my knees if they had asked me to. But of course they didn't, and I knew they wouldn't, and that just made it worse somehow. They didn't need to lay a hand on me. They just shuffled me off to bed crying and feeling so low and mean that I just lay there wide awake, thinking about what I had done and how I'd make it up to them. Geez.

Well, the 'Jays were bungling plays left and right, so I more or less had to listen to Georgie babble, and sure enough, he finally got around to Kirk's suicide. It had hit the papers the day before, and knowing how Georgie liked to mind everyone else's business but his own, I knew he'd bring it up sooner or later. He has his big schnozzola into everything.

I told him what he wanted to hear, all the gory details. The thing didn't surprise me – let me tell you that from the start. All those religious fanatics do either one of two things, martyr themselves early on in the game or live forever sponging money off old people who are afraid of rotting after they croak. Well, I knew old Amos didn't have the brains to get rich, so I wasn't too surprised when Pendoro walked into our room all glassy-eyed and said, "The prophet is dead." Cliff and I couldn't make any sense out of it, so we had him sit down (he really looked bad), but all he could do was sit there and mumble "The prophet is dead" and point out into the hall like he'd seen a ghost.

I finally realized that Kirk was about the closest thing to a prophet we had on the floor, so I moseyed out into the hall toward his room. I thought Pendoro was giving us his usual nonsense, so when I pushed the door open it gave me quite a start to see Kirk hanging from a steam pipe directly over an open Bible. God, it really gave me the creeps for a second – it looked like some kind of bizarre ritual with that Bible there, especially when I noticed that it was turned to the Book of Amos. His face was purple, and he looked dead, but I touched him to make sure. We'd trashed the room the night before (all in good fun, of course), and it was still pretty much in the same condition we'd left it in – overturned bed, books on the floor and so on. He had put his desk back right side up, and a piece of notebook paper caught my eye, placed exactly in the center of the desk. I told Finestein about the letter, and he lapped it up like a hungry dog.

I'm telling you, if you didn't keep these bartenders posted on every little bit of scuttlebutt, they'd probably dry up and blow away. And Georgie's one of the worst.

Well, I went back into my room and sat down and told Cliff what I had seen, so he went in to check it out for himself and then came back and sat down. There we all sat, staring at each other like bumps on a log. Pendoro kept talking about prophets, and Cliff looked like he was getting ready to blow chow at any moment. All of a sudden he pipes up with "We shouldn't have trashed his room last night".

And I said, "What difference does it make? You read the letter, didn't you? It was more than just that. I've got a feeling that that Fellowship bullshit went straight to his head." I suspected more, but I didn't say anything at the time. Then I'll be damned if Pendoro didn't start talking about "shattered myths" and "misguided idolatry" like he was delivering an oral presentation or something. But he was near the mark. I could feel it.

We called the cops and watched them take the body down. Kirk's head was at a crazy angle, and the air got kind of stuffy in there all of a sudden so I had to step out to get a breath of fresh air. They covered him with a sheet and carried him down to a big ambulance parked outside the hall door. A lot of people saw him being loaded into the car, and of course they thought that someone had just broken a leg or something like that. The dean called a meeting in our lounge a few days later to try to smooth things over, but it was already too late – everybody knew all about it by then. The only thing I wonder about is how many times this kind of thing has happened in the past, how many times some poor slob's mind has finally caved in at this place. Hell, nowadays these small schools will accept just about anybody – bi-polar, schizophrenic, or what-have-you. No wonder these people end up doing themselves in. I'm surprised I haven't done *myself* in by now.

At the orphanage they used to lay all that Christian horseshit on us, spoon-feeding it to us in the classroom and trying to warp our tender young minds by herding us into the sanctuary every day for worship. There was something about it that didn't sit right with me from the very beginning, though. I think it was because the altar boys and prefects would act so goddamned pious around the adults, but when they weren't being watched, they'd turn right around and start playing God around the rest of us small fry. There was this older kid that I used to hang out with, Rich Parker, who I thought was a halfway decent guy. We used to head to the bathroom to sneak a smoke between classes. This one time he had this felt-tip marker with him, and we started drawing stuff on the walls. I remember I went over to one of the stalls and wrote *The Spirit of God moves within me* right next to the crapper (which I thought was pretty clever, especially at that age) with Parker looking on and laughing like it was the funniest thing he had ever seen. The next day I was standing in the rector's office stammering out some dumb excuse and slowly realizing that my good friend Rich Parker had spilled his guts about the whole thing. Some friend.

Once in a while we'd all head downtown on Sunday for special masses. The nuns would round us up and stuff us into a school bus all dressed up in our nice little ties and monkey-suits. We'd have to sit quiet so that the sister could tell us what to do and what not to do, with me sitting there the whole time wishing I was back in bed or playing ball or doing anything else but riding around in some stuffy old bus listening to some stuffy old nun with her dos and don'ts and shoulds and shouldn'ts. Christ Almighty. I was only a little kid, after all, and what can a little kid do in a situation like that? At that age, I couldn't very well stand up and say, "Sister, I realize that your actions spring from only the best-intentioned of motives, but at this particular point in time my peers and I would prefer to be reflecting on matters of appreciably less importance than on those which I presume that we, though only nominal theists, are preparing to contemplate on this fine Sunday morning." Are you kidding? That's something Pendoro would say.

Compared to mass, the bus trip was a joyride. Watching some sweaty pedophile in a big ugly costume rant and rave about salvation, retribution, and ghosts is not my idea of a good time, and watching those poor suckers around me stuffing the coffers just to keep his pockets lined just about made me puke. I was truly happy to get away from all that.

I guess Amos was, too.

I started to think about all the things we'd done to Kirk during the school year and tried to feel guilty about them. I couldn't. If for just once he'd dropped the I'm-saved-you're-damned attitude, I think he would have been accepted. Pendoro said that Kirk had actually told him that, that he was saved and Pendoro was damned. He told him that when Judgment Day comes, he'll look over at him and cry because he'd tried to bring him into the fold, but he just wouldn't listen. And when Pendoro is thrown into the Lake of Fire, he'll wring his hands and beg God to save him, but it won't do any good because Pendoro was a lousy sinner just like the rest of us.

After all that he still expected to make friends here. He was a decent enough guy, and I happen to know that Pendoro liked him in spite of all his hellfire and damnation, but he refused to come down off his cross and mingle with us lesser creatures. And that's exactly why we played all those dumb pranks on him – we just wanted him to act like a normal human being. Instead, he treated us like dirt. What a chump.

Finestein had finally finished grilling me, and I had kind of fallen into a funk thinking about Kirk, when in walks my old pal Herb Munro, more or less alone. The sad thing about Herb is that he's a preppie and looks it – the sweater, the shoes, the haircut, the New England accent. He stands out in a crowd, he really does. He had Brad Landau in tow, a short dumpy kid with glasses from Pittsburgh. Munro takes him everywhere he goes just so he'll have someone around to agree with him all the time. They make quite a pair.

Herb saw me and Jo-Jo over at the bar, so he poked Landau in the ribs and sauntered over to where we were sitting.

"Why so glum, chum?" he said, talking to me. I told him to sit down and shut up. Finestein left to go tend to some business, so Munro and Munro II plopped down in stools right next to me, grinning twins.

"What's up, McDougal? You look like your mother just died," he said, trying his damnedest to keep from laughing. See what I mean? I figured the asshole didn't deserve any attention after that kind of crack, so I just stared at the counter in front of me, sipping my beer and pretending like he didn't exist. But he didn't let up.

"This isn't the McDougal I know. What happened to the guy with the ready retort?" He leaned forward and looked at Joe. "What wrong with your friend here, Finch?"

"I don't know. I haven't been able to get a word out of him. He just shut up all of a sudden."

"This is so unlike him. Perhaps a little bit of news will pull him out of it." He looked at me like a wolf. "I saw Prentiss today. He was walking toward the bus station with his duffel bag. I asked him where he was going, and the son of a bitch walked right past me like I wasn't even there."

"No shit?" said Jo-Jo.

"Yeah, no shit. I'll bet our friend McGossip here has details. Well, McDougal?"

I could have *sold* him the story, he was so anxious to hear about it. I looked over at the guy to make sure that he was for real. There were a few stories going around about old Herb too: expulsion from an Ivy League school because of plagiarism, academic probation, and so on and so forth. Preppie through and through. Maybe that's why he was so eager to hear about Prentiss – you know, the expulsion, the scandal, birds of a feather, all that. I knew the Prentiss story would get around anyway, and to tell you the truth, I'd been itching to get it off my tongue ever since I'd heard it from Pendoro. I filled the boys in.

"Herb," I said, putting my hand on his shoulder real buddy-buddy-like. "Our friend Prentiss is a queer. A fairy. A fag, a fruit, a homo. What do you think of that?"

I let them chew on that for a while, and while they were trying to believe it I downed the rest of my beer. I could hear Landau saying over and over again, "I don't fucking believe it. I don't fucking believe it." Finally Munro picks his jaw off his lap and starts begging me for the rest of it. "Details, McDougal, details!" he kept saying. I had him buy me another beer before I told him the tale, and a good one at that, how they'd found Prentiss in Rodgers' office doing God-knows-what and how they'd tried to hush it up, but word got to the dean's office so that Flaxton had to ask for a resignation from Rodgers, who gave it to him pronto and cleared out before the shit hit the fan.

"But what about Prentiss? They didn't force him to go, did they?" Munro asked, and I told him that Pendoro had said that he had had no reason for leaving, really, that his leaving in fact pointed a finger at him as well as at Rodgers. If he'd hung around, the whole thing would have probably blown over, though both of them should have known that that kind of shit wouldn't wash at a conservative Christian college like this one. (To tell you the truth, I really hadn't gotten all the facts straight from Pendoro, so I probably fouled it up a little bit in the telling. Prentiss may have gone both ways now that I think about it. Who knows? And who cares, really? He was already gone, and after all of his macho bullshit it made a much better story if he was strictly a flamer.)

Pendoro was holding out on me too, I could tell. What gets me is that the guy won't tell you anything straight anymore – you have to weed through all the bullshit to get to the facts. What really gives me the creeps nowadays is when he'll walk right past me in the hallway like he doesn't even recognize me. And you should see him with Hager when she walks across campus holding hands real lovey-dovey with her "Tommy dear" or "Tommy love", with Pendoro looking off into the trees like Jesus Christ himself is up there swinging in the branches while he ignores Hager entirely. I swear to God he's lost his mind. I mean, this is the same guy who's been after her ass for the better part of a year, but then once he has her, it's like she might as well be dead for all the attention he gives her. They're together all the time, but the zombie doesn't even give her the time of day.

I'll tell you one thing, though – I would have given my right nut to get her out of our room while she was still with Clifton. She'd wander in around eleven o'clock every night sniffing around for my roommate. "Is Clifton here?" she'd ask. "I was just walking by your room, and I just wanted to see if he was in," knowing full well that he was already in there primed and ready for another night of intense humping, with me lying in the next room listening to her grunting and moaning all night long until I could barely stand it. God, was I glad when she gave Cliff the shaft so I could finally get some sleep. The nightly fuckathons

144

were probably part of what drove Kirk to kill himself. I wouldn't be at all surprised.

But can Clifton (as we know him) exist without a steady girlfriend? Can he do without the steady squeeze for any length of time? Hell, no. No, he has to shack up with Susie after Hager jilts him just to soothe his bloated ego, has to cover up just so he won't look and feel like a complete fool. He must be incredibly insecure or something, like he needs her just so he can say to the world, "Hey, I'm laying So-and-So now. I'm screwing her lousy eyes out night after night." Big deal. So he has a hundred pounds of flesh he can poke around in every night. Who cares? I mean, has it changed him? Isn't he still the same Clifton who walked into my room on the very day he arrived telling me to take the outside room or else? Right off the bat I knew what I was in for – the midnight parade across my bedroom, the stupid giggling and thrashing around, the squeaking and shrieking, and the umpteen trips to the bathroom. It got me so worked up once that I nearly jumped Hager on her way to the john. What a life.

And you should see Cliff and Susie together. Sure, around the room it's all kissy-huggy-poo, but outside it's a whole different story. Clifton treats her like shit, like a lapdog, just like he treated Hager only she was too interested in her split ends to pay any attention to her own dignity. What gets me is that Susie knows she's getting treated badly, and she *hates* it, but she doesn't do anything about it. I really can't figure it out at all, the way he talks down to her and gets away with it. If I were a chick, I'd pop him one right in the jewels and tell him to go to hell, the lousy bastard. She's an odd one, though. I've seen her warm up to so many guys, then turn cold on them as soon as they start going for it. In my particular case, I can't say that I actually fell for her completely, but I remember that we met down in the lounge one afternoon and seemed to hit it off pretty well – you know, the usual small talk and body games. What I liked about her was her sense of humor. She didn't take anything too seriously, including herself, which scored bonus points with me right away.

That's what's wrong with a lot of people around here – they take themselves far too seriously. It's dangerous in a way because it gets tough to roll with the punches – it gets real easy to get crushed. Take Munro, for example. He'd probably be an OK guy if he didn't take all that pre-law crap so seriously, locking himself in his room late at night pretending that he's poring over those big legal tomes he keeps around so he can impress his many friends (fill in "Landau" here). Then again, he's such a complete bung-hole that he's probably beyond help. Bad example.

Anyway, Quent and I started spending some time together going to movies and concerts and other things on campus. I'd go down to visit her once in a while, and we'd go walking over to Mollens Park to chew face and fondle. We also talked. She'd tell me about her hometown, which was kind of interesting in its own way since I'm from a big city and know absolutely zero about the rural part of the country. We talked quite a bit, and I liked it, but you know how easy it is to get sick of just talking, so I decided to bring things to a head, as it were. I sneaked down to her room one night around midnight and knocked on her door.

She opened it and let me in, and before you know it (and keep this under your hat), innocent Ian became a man in the fullest sense of the word. Jesus, it was really something. But I guess I must have stuck my foot in my mouth because when it was all over and done with and we were lying there basking in the afterglow, having wallowed in the swamp of salaciousness and all that, I leaned over and kissed her on the nose and said "Thanks", which was exactly what I was supposed to do, or so I thought. The second that word left my mouth I would have paid five bucks (maybe ten) to take it back because she froze up all of a sudden like a human icicle and wouldn't say a word to me the rest of the night or ever since, for that matter. Is that weird or what? Women.

Finch and Munro were talking about some guy in Jones Hall named Nabronski.

"Kicked out?" Jo-Jo was saying.

"Yeah," Munro said. "He walked into her room and tried to insert a baseball bat into the other guy's mouth – I can't remember his name right now. I guess he caught them with their pants down…" (we ignored the pun) "…and she was hitting Nabronski on the head with her fists while Nabronski was sitting on the other guy's chest trying to stretch his jaw open even more so he could slip the entire bat down there. In the meantime the room was filling up with people that lived on her floor, but not one of them laid a hand on the big Polack, and I don't blame them. He was roaring, and she was screaming. The other guy was whimpering and gurgling. It must have been something to see."

"So what happened?" I said, asking the obvious question.

"What happened? Nabronski succeeded in getting the bat halfway down his throat before the resident advisor stepped in and put a stop to the whole thing. Immediate expulsion. What I can't understand is how he got away with it scot-free. The guy is obviously off his nut, but he got away with a clean slate. He might as well have transferred."

Money, I thought. That's all it takes. *Money.* Little rich kids with their daddies ready to paper over their mistakes with a thick roll of C-notes. I see it every day.

Biffer came over to fill us up again, and talk of Kirk led eventually to mandatory church attendance, which everybody, including yours truly, thinks is a big crock of shit.

"There's no official church affiliation any longer, so why should we have to go?" the preppie was saying. He was right, although we had heard it all a hundred times before. "They're talking about pushing something through the student government if they can get enough support."

I had nothing to say that I hadn't said before. Landau chimed in with his nerdy "That's damned right!", and Jo-Jo said something about not minding having to sit through an hour of it once a week.

"I mean, after all, they used to hold chapel every single day. Imagine that. It's bad enough having to listen to Ritter once a month."

And I suddenly realized that that was why I was so down in the mouth. It was Ritter.

It didn't take too long after the suicide before I went to see him about Kirk. I knew where he lived, and I was prepared to beat the living shit out of him because I knew that he had had something to do with it, and I knew that if that was true he wouldn't have the guts to come out and admit it. I just wanted to help him get it off his chest, even if I had to remove his fucking head in the process. I really didn't know what I was going to say to him, and as it turned out, I didn't have to say much at all. It was almost like he was waiting for me.

I didn't even knock – I just walked right in. His place looked like a shrine, a monk's cell. Ritter was bent over his desk, "a scribe copying prophets' ravings", as Pendoro would say. He looked up, and I knew then and there that there was no sense in talking to him, no sense at all. I asked him if he'd heard about Kirk.

"Amos?" he said. He looked down and started writing again. "Oh yes. Very unfortunate."

The Highland temper was not there, my friends – I wasn't angry at all. In fact, it was pity I felt. I actually felt sorry for the poor son of a bitch.

"Did you kill him, Ritter?"

He knew what I meant. He looked up at me from his study table. I was a roach, an invader. If he could have crushed me then, he would have.

"No," he said. "I snapped at him. Nothing more. I'm sorry to have disappointed you."

I remember standing there smiling for a long time after that, smiling at his face of stone. For a long time I just stood there hating him, but not hating him so that I wanted to take his life as he had taken Kirk's. I hated Ritter so badly then that I wanted to do nothing more than to leave him alone in his miserable little cubicle, all by himself in his monk's cell, in his own isolated little hell. When I walked out of his room, I was satisfied.

But I can't help thinking now: *Should I have done more for Amos? Why did I always needle the poor bastard? We all killed him, didn't we?*

"McDougal." Munro was poking me in the ribs. "It's your round."

I reached absentmindedly into the wrong pocket for money and came out with a piece of paper, folded. It was that stupid poem that Pendoro gave me after he devoured all my cookies. While Biffer set us up again, I crumpled it up into a ball and threw it toward a trash can in the corner, easily a twenty-footer.

Three points.

IV

Tiny arms flailed at the platen. He stopped and, bending nearer, adjusted a lamp so that the light fell squarely on the limp page:

Sonnet (Fragmented) for a Magyar Crone

Once, in an earlier lifetime, beyond
The crumbling ramparts of our citadel,
We were told of a distant haven long
Since estranged from the war-gutted hell
That we call our homeland, our forsaken
And barren land bereft of corn and cow:
Blasted by the North in winter, and baked
By summer winds beneath our useless plows.

We were told that one of our ancient kings
(There were many) once traveled to that tame
Land bearing a chest full of gold rings,
Hoping to strike up a profitable trade:
He never returned.

By night now we crouch
By our watchfires, gaming for kings' crowns.

OK, I guess. This one escapes the pyre. The typewriter chattered defiantly as he jerked the sheet free of the carriage. He held it to the lamp, allowing the light to permeate the grouped characters, the cheap yellow paper. *Phoenix fixed on foolscap: palimpsests of images of ideas of concepts of abstractions of perceptions. My poetry, which Prentiss derided, fleeing. Both gone now – St. Stephen, St. Amos.* His eyes fell on another scrap of paper nearby:

Once, Boo Rainmaker stole a summer day from his brother Sol;
Laughing, Boo stole it and made it rain.
And Haymaker Sol wept to see the flowers droop,
Their proud faces bent obediently to Boo, his impish brother.

151

He slumped forward in his chair and let the paper fall to the floor by his feet. Dust devils leaped and settled. *Ruth's hair: her dingy hair all over my dusty floor. What will she say? What will everyone else say?* His hands fell in two flaccid piles on the desktop. *And what do I know? Given: "Knowledge is the summation of experience, with each succeeding year describing a progressively smaller part of that experience. This in turn effects a distorted perception of time, a temporal diminution or acceleration, so that near life's end one scarcely has time to ponder an afterlife." Eloquently rendered. Pendoro the Pendoro.*

His fingers discovered a balled-up slip of pink paper on the desktop. He carefully unfolded it and smoothed it against a textbook. He rested his chin on the typewriter. *Dear Mr. Pendoro: The Office of Academic Affairs regrets to inform you that...* It shrank softly into the palm of his hand as he crushed it tightly. *Get thee gone. "We had such great hopes for you, Tommy, our poor, poor black sheep." Ah Mama, Papa – they had nothing to teach me here. "What's Tommy doing these days, T.P.?" "You're asking ME? I've disowned the ungrateful son of a..."*

Father?

Yes? (Rattles newspaper. Oblivious.)

Father?

Yes? What IS it, child? (Irritated now. Folds paper in lap. Tamps tobacco.)

Do you remember that I'm in college now?

Remember? (Hrmmphs.) Do I remember, do you say? I should say I do. Your mother – may God damn her soul – and I have always had great hopes for you ever since we learned of your exceptionally high I.Q., and I do mean exceptionally high...

Vagaries attendant on genius?

Don't interrupt. Now, as I was saying, being fully aware of your intellectual capabilities, I have never had the slightest doubt that you will succeed. The world is your oyster, boy – you hold it in the palm of your hand...

(Produce pink slip. Offer.) That's what I wanted to talk to you about. You see...

Yes, we knew, your mother and I. You're grown up now, aren't you? Fifteen or sixteen, if my memory serves me correctly?

Eighteen, Dad...

Grown up. A man. So I guess you're old enough to know now: you're really not our child after all. I think we either adopted you or bought you on the black market. Or maybe you were born illegitimately, a bastard – I really don't recall at the moment. Your mother (that is, your foster mother) pulled the wool over my eyes. Barren. Had I been royalty (and who's to say that I'm not?), I would have dumped her on the spot. By the way, you really can't imagine all the trouble involved in removing lipstick from lapels, all of that. You'll find out soon enough, I daresay. When you grow up.

But…

The bitch claimed that it was the drinking that drove her away. But SHE was the one that got me started in the first place. It's like someone getting angry at you because SHE kicked YOU in the stones. Can you make any sense out of that woman? To make matters worse, there was that worthless son of mine who thought that he was better than I was. Did I raise a son to be better than his own father? I finally had him sent off to Scranton…

Flanders, Pop.

You again? What are you doing here? Aren't you supposed to be with your mother this weekend? (Pulls flask out of bathrobe. Looks around nervously before drinking.) She's not here now, is she?

I have come to tell you that the college has suspended me.

Our pride and joy. A serendipity! (Inhales deeply with pride, exhales loudly.) My father called them superior genes, the Pendoro strain. Generations of success. Doctors, lawyers, statesmen. A pillar of the community, every one of them. My grandfather was proud of my father, and my father was just as proud of me as I am of Tommy. Bring 'em up right, give 'em a good education, and let those genes do the rest. (Drinks deeply.) My boy!

My father.

Eh? (Looks up, frightened and defensive.) Heroic flaw, right? A little booze never hurt anyone. And you can't question my professional work: it's impeccable. Sons of bitches, all of them. I needs me a drink… Tommy? Come here, you egghead – I'm going out. I want this place cleaned up by the time I get back, and make sure those dishes are done. But in case you decide to go out and assert your manhood for a change, here's a little money to go buy your ladyfriend something with. (Offers a handful of loose change. Laughs.) Later.

Godspeed.

He rose suddenly and, stepping to the window, lifted a corner of the shade. He pushed his nose against the glass. *Silly boy, you left the shade down all day long. See you at the union, Snuggle Bunny. Eightish be fine? Lovely! Can't wait! See you then! Bubble, bubble. Pendoro, what have you done?*

"*But you couldn't have known.*"

But I did.

"*Such nice hair…*"

Raven wisps, gossamer fine.

"*And green eyes…*"

Emeralds.

"*Pug nose…*"

Cute as a button.

"*Coy smile…*"

Enticing, yes.

"*Full lips…*"

Yes, indeed.

"*Nice breasts…*"

Ski slopes.

"*Pert derrière…*"

The pertest on campus.

"*Tapered legs…*"

Veritable balusters they are.

"*And nicely dressed.*"

A paragon. Dressed for any occasion.

"*So what's wrong?*"

"I don't know," he said under his breath. Moisture spread and faded on the windowpane. *It too leaves, leaving no trace.* He walked slowly to the next room and leaned his weight against the jamb.

"*You do not have to leave,*" I said. "*No one is making you go. It will pass,*" I said. "*Let it alone.*"

He lay with his duffel bag beside him on the bed, silent bedfellow. "At this place? It won't pass, Pendoro. It travels with me. I took it to sea with me. They found me out and kicked my ass out of the navy, and now I have to leave college because some asshole walked into Rodgers' office without knocking." The cigarette hung from his lower lip as it always had, as if he was telling everyone to go to hell. "What gets me is that people thought I was the all-American boy." Ash fell to his chest as he began to laugh. Even you, the guy who's supposed to know everything, couldn't figure it out. Maybe it was too simple for you, Pendoro. Have you ever thought of that? Maybe it was just a little bit too simple even for you to figure out." Laughter shook his chest, rattled the bed and floor. It stopped, and his eyes opened.

"Where to now?" I asked him. He ignored the question and rose from his bunk, digging around in his duffel bag so that he could prolong the moment.

"I'll go home for a while. I haven't seen my family for a long time. Maybe they've missed me or something. Maybe they haven't. I'll see." He stood ready to go. "Maybe I'll even tell them what I've been doing for the past three years. Who knows? My brothers and sisters still write to me sometimes, so I guess they can't hate me." He moved toward the door, and when he dropped his bag we shook hands gravely. He said, "I'll miss you, Tommy," then picked up his gear again without looking back, through his door and my door and gone. Gone.

"And I miss you too, Prentiss, but the words weren't there. I couldn't even tell you goodbye." His empty words echoed in an empty room.

The odor of cheap perfume filled his nose, and he turned, coughing. Ruth Hager lay spreadeagled on his bed dressed only in bracelets and rhinestone slippers. She lay eating from a box of chocolates and looked up languidly as Tommy moved toward the foot of the bed. Chocolate smeared her lips. She continued eating, speaking to Tommy out of the side of her mouth: "Oh, Tommy dear, will you run get Mama a glass of water? She's gotten this nasty chocolate all over herself. You're such a dear."

Tommy turned automatically to obey. "Oh, and Tommy..." He halted. "I've heard that you've been associating with bi-sexuals." She wagged a reproachful finger at him. "Mommy doesn't like that at all. It just won't do for Tommy to be seen with nasty little fruitcakes. Do you hear me?" He felt a need to say something in his behalf. "But I...," he blurted, then turned meekly to do her bidding.

He closed and opened his eyes, scattering the image.

Of course I will have to tell her. There's no way to get around it. She will not understand. How can I expect her to understand?

Goodbye, Steven.

A breeze lifted the curtains opposite him, and the sun shaped lattices on the floor beside him. *Voices drifted in from the quadrangle. "Did we win the football game, Prentiss?"* Outside the smell of dead leaves

rose from sodden clumps on the pavement below his window. "Did we?"
Gaudy leaves in distant fields, the harvest season. Sharp-scented apples and
laughing, ruddy-faced girls in hay wagons. His heart fell. "Did we?"
Behind him Prentiss' books fell loudly to his desk.

"How the hell should I know, Pendoro? Don't you think I have any-
thing better to do?" Neither cared. His hand left a foggy imprint on the glass
and faded.

Tommy stared out the window. The sun shone somewhere
behind the intersection of two crossbars. He felt strangely
saddened by its absence and diverted his eyes to the warm golden
lattice at his feet. *Four crucifixes: one for my Master, two for the petty*
thieves at Golgotha, and one for the dead boy who lived down the hall. Ian
with his prophecies: "I saw it coming, Pendoro. I told you so." Perhaps…

"Do you ever think about girls, Tommy?" His eyes followed mine.
"Have you ever kissed one?" My hands interested me suddenly – I could
not face him. "Do you think Ruth likes me, Tommy? I mean, what if I
bought her a present or something? What do you think? I think I love her,
Tommy." Pariah. Misfit.

He spat on the floor.

In the pantry they had sat alone together in the darkness, breathing in
the faint odor of damp cardboard. He sat alone, a boy of twelve, feeling her
presence beside him, feeling her voice brush soft words across his face. Her
touch thrilled him, the touch of a girl whom he had teased tirelessly for
years, throwing acorns at her and pulling her hair. She had slowly begun to
change, though – he could sense that. And he had changed too, for he
allowed the soft fingers to touch him freely. He shivered and remained
completely still. The hands thrilled him, yet he could not explain why. He
wanted very much to move closer to her so that his body could touch hers,
but he didn't.

The mechanics of sex repelled him, and he forcibly tried to couple the
sense of her touch with the pictures he had once seen in an old magazine,
but he couldn't. It confused him. When the hands moved timidly from his
face toward his waist, he shivered so violently that he grew afraid and
crawled away from her to a darker corner, out of her reach. He felt
threatened by her nearness, as if he had some awful secret whose discovery
would destroy him. He felt that it lay terribly exposed to her probing fingers,
and he feared that she would find it and take it from him. But there was no
secret. And he trusted her enough to believe that she would not take it from

him even if it existed. He waited a long time for her to leave. When she left, he tried to sort out his thoughts, but all he could do was to gaze vacantly at the weak light draining through the keyhole...

But it's not the same – there is no closeness between us. We share nothing. He pulled his eyes from the floor and walked swiftly to the lavatory. The water sang soothingly in his cupped hand, and he bent to drink. He shut his eyes and let the water wet his lips and dribble into the sink. *Like her lips. Cold. Very cold.*

To: Ms. Ruth Hager
From: Thomas Pendoro
Re: A desultory engagement to have commenced at
*   approximately 8:00 p.m. on April 27th*

Dear Ms. Hager:

I regret to inform you that I will be unable to meet you this evening as planned. I further regret that any postponement of such an engagement becomes highly unlikely in light of my recent suspension from Flanders College.

Have a great year.

Sincerely, etc.

He sat down on Prentiss' bare mattress and buried his face in his hands. Again, as he had months earlier, he felt the approaching night calling him, the sweet succor of darkness spreading from the outermost fringes of his soul to its very core. He felt depraved. He had given of himself innocently before the image of his own desire only to be repudiated, cast aside as something lacking worth or validity. Tommy the poet had presented himself to an exalted being and had been rejected, but not entirely. She had accepted him on terms far distant from those he had anticipated: where he had wished for a union of souls, he had received only a union of flesh, a tenuous relationship resting on little more than appearances. He imagined himself looking through the eyes of Ruth Hager at an image of herself in a large looking glass. Her naked beauty intimidated him as he watched the girl bend down gracefully to pick up a small hand mirror from her night table. He trembled. Her thoughts became suddenly audible to him, and he cringed, repulsed by their crude banality.

He recalled the evening after Amos' suicide when they had sat side by side on a bench looking toward Fowler Hall. He had had little to say and had permitted her words to rush past him without interruption. Their callousness numbed him. Amos was dead, and the full awareness of his death had struck him dumb in the face of the incessant flow of trivialities. He asked himself frankly what she had found so interesting in him that she had been willing to jilt Clifton for a new relationship. He did not know, and the answer lay on his conscience like some oppressive burden which he found hopelessly incapable of removing. He had spoken grudgingly in reply to her question:

"I don't want to do anything tonight, Ruth. Nothing at all."

And he had again seen and ignored the look of contempt that darkened her eyes, her lovely jaded eyes.

I will not go. It has continued far too long.

He unlocked his fingers and lifted his eyes wearily to the half-open window gaping like a fading portal in front of him. A thin rosy corona of light outlined a distant building as the sun set behind it. Students' voices rose and fell, and he felt drawn to them.

There was no escape. Around him sat countless clusters of students murmuring quietly. Expectation tinged their voices, but he sat quietly. Images of the snowy Missouri countryside that Finch had often described to him flitted endlessly through his mind, and he longed for the winter air. He knew that the air would sparkle, that it would be cold and bright outside. A platform had been set against one side of the large room, and professors, men and women of learning, most of whom he recognized, paced importantly back and forth. He became nervous suddenly and felt the first secretion of sweat dampen his face.

And it was too warm. Outside the air would be cold, and he could imagine the rows of black trees and fence-posts extending and receding into the fresh white fields. He gripped his coat around him and moved to leave. Someone tugged at his sleeve, and he turned. A slender youth with ashen eyes greeted him, and Tommy, after a moment's reflection, recognized him and returned the greeting. He had sat next to him in algebra class, a thin chalk-faced boy. It was P.

"I've read your poem, Pendoro," he said nervously. His eyes glanced distractedly at a girl sitting beside them. "It's excellent. You stand an excellent chance, you know."

A tall dark-suited figure, a professor, approached the platform. Thoughts of Linda Arenson agitated him – he had seen her sitting near the door as he entered, and the presence of the boy now only piqued his agitation. The idle flattery dismayed him, and he felt completely removed from his surroundings, as though he were looking at himself and the large room filled with students through a narrow lens. The mention of his poem brought a fresh effusion of sweat to his face; he felt flushed in the stifling atmosphere, and his whole body ached. Although he was not facing a window, he was certain that it was snowing outside. He squirmed and looked away from the boy, hoping to evade his idle praise. The dark-suited professor picked his way nimbly through the crowd, mounted the platform, and positioned himself behind a microphone perched over a thin wooden lectern. The room quieted.

"I'd like to begin," he said, "by giving you a brief history of this contest. It occurs annually, every January, after the students have returned from Christmas break. The interim gives the judges a chance to study the poems carefully so as to give all contestants their just due. Each contestant is allowed to enter as many as three poems, although this is eventually narrowed to one as the competition progresses. Of all the poems entered – one hundred and fifty-nine this year – four are picked for final judging. Money is awarded to the top three contestants, and a small plaque is given to the fourth-place finisher. All judges are members of the Flanders English department."

Tommy let the voice drone and dwindle. The prospect of winning made him feel cheapened, and the thought of so many eyes passing over his precious wordhoard like some shiny bauble aroused in him a miser's possessiveness. He had yielded to mistaken judgment: he had permitted pride to rule his actions. Shame burned his face as he listened and watched the runners-up recite their own strings of verse and blush with their own bloated self-esteem. Fragments of his own poem floated like jagged shards before him, now broken and worthless. His mind moved again to the protective image of the snow-quilted fields, and the vision of the countryside with the tiny farmhouses winking warmly in the midst of so much desolation comforted him.

By a stranger's door will I lay me down…

"Thomas Pendoro…" *His name startled him out of his reverie. Beside him the pale boy fixed him with an invidious stare as applause erupted in Tommy's ears and mind. He fumbled at the floor with his hands and pushed himself to his feet, wavering in the carnival atmosphere. His thoughts rebelled, and he shuffled reluctantly toward the platform, thinking:* Why did I do this? Why? *A hand slipped into his at the lectern, and he shook it weakly, feeling a sheet of paper being thrust into his other hand. It felt slick to his touch, slick and faintly unctuous. He quailed at the task in front of him.*

Why?

The microphone pointed at him like a cold blue finger. The words were his, not theirs, and the thought of sharing them seemed abhorrent to him. The poem was too personal, too large a part of him to share it with the herded faces which had suddenly frozen into an attitude of polite anticipation. He did not know them, nor they him. He wanted to leave.

He stood momentarily in the backwash of their favor, an unlikely champion of artistic expression, and the realization left a brackish film on his wounded conscience. It was only when a hand touched his elbow that he stepped to the lectern and looked down at the slick page in his sweating hands, his child. He thought of the pleasure its creation had given him, the moments spent shaping the myriad words which the idea evoked into an expression succinct and trenchant. It filled his heart with a simple joy reminiscent of his childhood. But the words were his alone – a public recitation, a public spectacle would corrupt the untainted quality of his work. A flame roared in his head: there was no escape. He looked down at the title and read aloud:

Aurelius in Carnuntum…

He had slurred the words badly. Aurelius the dutiful Stoic, *he thought.* "Living in accordance with Nature." So do I really belong here? *He swallowed and continued:*

> *We marched down other roads before*
> *When, as a younger man, I saw the past*
> *Merge with the future, my dreams coming last,*
> *Stretching in desolate parallels or*
> *Lingering in the eyes of old whores*
> *Or ringing like bright coins in a child's song*

> *Sung to a tune of its own making, strong*
> *And untroubled by thoughts of false honor.*
> *This I have seen. Roads have since begun*
> *And ended, thin tenuous strips of field*
> *Fading under yellow skies or shining*
> *With a dull glory beneath a dead sun*
> *As my lodestar, nor do I so easily feel*
> *Comfort in a cave where the nymphs sing.*

Applause, noxious and unrestrained, pierced the air. He leaned shaking arms against the lectern and rested his chin on his chest.

I have betrayed my ideals, *he thought.* And for what?

An envelope appeared, attached to a cuff-linked hand.

For Mammon?

A fresh wave of hand-clapping assailed him. He looked out into the crowd.

For them? So I thought at one time.

His feet led him away. The noise around him ebbed, and a bittersweet emptiness filled his spirit and washed away the remaining shame of his exhibitionism. He could go now – it was all over.

Tommy stood up and stepped slowly to the window. Below he could see students strolling lazily through the still spring evening and the lengthening shadows across the quadrangle. He pined for his lost youth – the years had robbed his life of its freshness. He felt the lonely mantle of age pressing upon his shoulders as he looked out at the dying day.

She jilted him because of the contest, for a new image. Before then I was nothing to her. Poet and ingenue. Christ. Alarm seized him briefly, and he caught his breath. *Did I rescue it from the flames for Ruth Hager?* He relaxed and watched a lamp illuminate a room at the far end of the quadrangle. No, he had written the poem for himself and for others like him – of that he was sure. The assurance consoled him, and a strong sense of resolution beckoned him away. A flock of swallows darted like scraps of tin in the evening sky, and in the distance the chapel bells began to toll. When the seventh bell sounded he turned from the window: the spring night lay waiting.

He closed the door quietly behind him and walked down the hallway to the stairs. Clifton sat on the banister, and Tommy could feel his friend's indignation follow him down the first flight of steps. As he turned at the landing he looked up briefly at the lone figure seated on the railing above him. Clifton's eyes flashed their contempt, eyes of a spurned lover.

He jostled him roughly.

"What the fuck are you doing with my girl, Pendoro?"

He did not feel threatened. He was not at all concerned for his safety – the hands would free him soon. He had no reply, and Clifton knew it, and while he groped for words Clifton released his shirt. Tommy relaxed, seeing resignation in the other's downcast face.

"Are you referring to Ruth or Susie, Clifton? Or to both?"

For him Ruth had dropped Clifton. For Clifton Susie had dropped no one. For no one Susie had dropped Clifton, and he, Tommy, was left with Ruth while Clifton was left out in the cold. It made him dizzy to think about it. A hand squeezed his shoulder.

"I'm sorry, Tommy."

He stopped and looked up. Clifton looked away, and Tommy's heart sank.

They had once been friends, and the supreme irony of the situation shaped his lips into a faint smile.

If only you knew.

Clifton had changed recently. Since Susie had left him he had become more pensive, and even though Clifton still refused to speak to him, Tommy realized that the two jiltings, one which was as yet unexplained and the other which in retrospect seemed more and more like a senseless act of capriciousness, had proved beneficial in the end. For Clifton, who had spent his whole life using others to further his own ends, had at last reached a sort of impasse at which his emotions, following in the wake of his headlong journey through the lives of others, had finally washed over and past him and back again and again. It had humbled him. Even his tone of voice had assumed a diffidence unusual for him. Tommy wondered silently if he too had changed. He thought not.

"Hi, Clifton."

Clifton looked down at his hands folded in his lap. A wry smile split his face as he turned his head toward Tommy below him.

"How ya doin', Tommy?" he drawled. *The affection in his voice brightened the air as Clifton rose and slid down the banister to where he was standing.*

"What's up, Pendoro?"

It could not be – he did not return his greeting. Pride would not yet allow him to do so, the old pride which had all but destroyed him. Clifton's face was drawn and haggard; his hair was unkempt and matted, clinging in a rude tangled mass to the sides of his head; he was unshaven, and his muscles, once hard and well defined, hung flaccidly from his limp arms. He had been ravaged by an excess of self-pity, his spirits dulled by a surfeit of remorse.

He awaits my departure, as I await his dismissal. He railed at the walls once and kept McDougal awake; now he lets it rankle when once he would have flattened me without stopping to think about it. He continued to stand at the landing, studying the peeling molding which curled at his feet. He thought suddenly of Clifton's mother and the way he had once described her to him: a tired woman who had managed to deliver two strong children, a prodigal son and a daughter who seemed to be Clifton's conscience. *You more than anyone else should realize that it doesn't matter. We all muddle through.*

Clifton's soles grated harshly against marble as he swung his legs from the banister to the floor.

"Wait, Clifton."

He froze and seemed to hesitate. Tommy climbed a step and retreated again to the landing. Clifton stood rigidly at right angles to him, a single bulb illuminating his disheveled hair. The steps, each worn smooth by the procession of years, rose infinitely before Tommy's eyes to where his friend stood, Clifton, who encompassed all the faults and virtues of the endless line of men and women who had preceded him. In the weak light Tommy could discern a tragic profile, and the young voices which sang out suddenly from below echoed voices of a past day.

"It's over, Clifton. Ruth and I are through."

It was not difficult to imagine. In his mind he saw them walking to class, her coterie walking briskly to class and fouling the sweet morning air with innuendoes directed at each other and at anyone else in the vicinity. Nothing of any substance would dare to enter their conversation. A velvet, sunlit breeze would caress her dark tresses in its warm richness, and a squirrel would bound playfully across her path; fresh leaves would shimmer softly in the trees, reflecting her green eyes; a thick smell of clipped grass, the fragrance of spring, would linger in the air, and birds would flit from branch to branch above. But all would be lost on her. Her beauty, striving to spread and unite with the natural beauty surrounding her, would drop instead like a garish pall upon the heads and shoulders of her friends, who were in many ways nothing more than spurious imitators. A shrill voice, divested of any human interest, would interrupt and pry briefly. And she:

"Who? Tommy Pendoro? No, you have it all wrong, dear."

"It really doesn't matter, Pendoro," Clifton said. He gripped the door to the hallway in one hand, the banister in the other. "Our friendship was far more important than that, anyway. You know that." *Our friendship. Was.*

Water covered the floor of the hallway. McDougal shouted from the far end with his pants rolled up to his knees.

"Don't be a wimp, Pendoro. Be a man for once in your life."

"You mean, if I crack my head open, I'm a man?"

"Yeah, that's how it works." He kicked the water impatiently. "C'mon. We're all waiting on you."

He sighed and began to roll up the cuffs of his pants. He had heard water in the hallway earlier but had ignored it, trying to concentrate on a textbook over the noise of McDougal's stereo blaring out into the corridor. When the water began to seep under his door, he finally opened it and watched McDougal skid on a thin plane of water to the opposite end of the hallway. Prentiss stepped out from behind him and leaned wearily against the wall. He reached for a cigarette.

"What the hell is the asshole up to now?" he asked.

Clifton emerged from his room and shook his head at the water.

"How did you get all this water out here, Mac?"

"I let the tub overflow in the bathroom." He tapped his forehead and grinned. "Ingenious, is it not?"

Clifton ignored him and looked down the hall at Tommy.

"Are you going to try this, Pendoro?"

"McDougal says I'm not a man if I don't."

"Let me try first," he said, walking carefully to where Prentiss was standing.

"How about you, Prentiss?"

"Do you think I'm crazy?"

"Well, move aside, then." He backed up a few paces. "Here goes." He leaped forward in small and then larger strides. Halfway down the hall he brought his feet together and glided gracefully to where McDougal sat jeering at him.

"Attaboy, jocko. Right on your ass. That's the way."

Bradley Landau's head poked out into the hallway and turned turtle-like from side to side.

"What the hell's going on here? What's all this commotion? What's all this water doing on the floor?"

"Just shut up and get out of the way, you idiot," McDougal said. "Pendoro's getting ready to fall on his ass." Landau pulled his head in from the doorway.

Tommy pushed himself away from the wall and sprinted out onto the slippery floor... and gazed up at a circle of swollen faces grouped far above him like brooding clouds. A hand fell from the sky and cradled his head. It was Clifton. In the distance he could hear voices:

"He fell on his ass. I knew he would."

"Shut up for once, McDougal."

"He's bleeding a little. I think it's a concussion."

A handkerchief dabbed his mouth. He had fallen and hurt himself. The handkerchief was Clifton's.

"He'll be all right."

He felt Clifton's strong hand cupped under his head lying in the water. The water was warm, and he floated beneath a circle of clouds, supported by Clifton's hand which had fallen from the sky to save him. He felt very drowsy.

"I'm going to call an ambulance."

Ambulance. His vision cleared suddenly, and he looked up at Clifton, whose face swelled and shrank in rhythm to his flurried heartbeat.

"Clifton."

"You're going to be OK, Pendoro."

His eyes showed confidence, two distinct points of confidence in a nebulous milky haze. The words sank like small pebbles, and tranquillity followed them into his receding consciousness. Only the eyes remained, full of fire and stars.

Two doors barred his vision where Clifton had passed. Loud voices hailed and passed him, their gestures crude and insolent.

Profaners. A fart flapped moistly, and laughter followed. Tommy looked up beyond them to the head of the stairs.

Desiderata.

Clifton had surmounted his desiderata. *Rise, pass, and fall.* Roughspoken louts, usurpers, followed to succeed their fallen king. Gaunt, gowned apparitions passed on the stairs, ghosts of an earlier day, and a cold draft chilled the sweating stone. His fingers reached to stroke its dampness. Closed doors barred his way, doors which now separated him from Clifton, who had in turn separated himself from the ghastly parade to observe its pallid anonymity, to reflect. *Reflect.* Generation upon generation in unbroken sequence, a dreary concatenation of linked lives like his own.

His spirit writhed and lay still, exhausted. He longed for the detached numbness his solitude had once won him, the sweet coolness of the night. *Reflect.* Clifton had glimpsed the squalor of his own soul – they shared a common horror now and could never be friends again. A door had opened and closed forever between them. The others had also passed by him, and their rude passage evoked his own chastened vanity. It sickened him.

He has changed. Have I?

With his eyes closed he could hear Prentiss snorting. *"You, Pendoro? Change? Listen, man, the only way you'll ever change is if you find some woman to pull you down to earth, and I'll tell you something: that Hager bitch ain't the one."* He stepped quickly down the stairs.

He did not confront Ruth Hager at the hall door – he passed freely out into the night. *Her lovely, jaded, contemptuous eyes.* The quadrangle was empty, and the unshaded lamps on the wall, which had so often reminded him of a penal institution, outlined cracked mortar and cast a thin glow on the concrete in front of him. Ahead, the globe lamps sputtered at the darkness. There was no one in sight.

All at the movie.

Dogs barked in the distance, and he paused to listen. Crickets sang in the grass nearby, and he stepped from the sidewalk to the grass and squatted, listening. A car growled in the street and the crickets stopped. He waited, but it remained silent, and after several moments he rose and shuffled toward the street with his hands in his pockets.

"I do not think that they will sing to me..."

But the falling night welcomed him. He could see the stars beginning to sparkle in the evening sky, and he could hear the wind blowing softly in the trees, his favorite sound. He could feel the evening against his face like a cool, damp cloth, and he could taste its sweetness. He turned and followed a street which ran alongside the campus. Lights twinkled gaily in the windows.

Amos' breath rose in pointless clouds.

"Well, if you don't believe in God, then what do you believe in?"

They had wrangled for an hour in the cold, and Tommy wanted to go inside. If they walked faster, maybe...

"I don't believe in anything worth relating, Amos. We live in the Age of the Skeptic."

Amos stuck his jaw out like a stubborn bulldog. A wide scarf hung from his neck to his knees, an angry plaid. He waved a handful of stubby fingers in the air.

"OK. Suppose there isn't a God. Then how do you explain all of this?" His arms swept around and behind them, gathering in the trees, the snow, the warm houses. Tommy paraphrased in a monotone:

"The concept of beginning and ending is a purely human one, an anthropocentrism." The word danced lightly on his tongue. "It is presumptuous to extrapolate from a micro- to a macrocosm. Creation, like the notion of any deity, was fabricated to satisfy our passion for explanation. That does not preclude the existence of a divine being, nor does it vindicate one."

The words were stale, a stock passage out of any given philosophy textbook. He had countered Amos' arguments at first with enthusiasm, hoping to sway him. He had realized gradually, however, that Amos was too embedded in his own beliefs to listen to new ideas. He had tried to direct Amos' thinking to obvious inconsistencies by a line of leading questions, but Amos would elude him by quoting Biblical passages, begging the question. Now Tommy was only repeating himself. And it was cold. They both walked on noisily through the packed snow. He had little trouble sensing Amos' pity – he had tried to save his friend Tommy from certain damnation and had failed. They would be nearing the campus soon. He decided to change the subject:

"Are your grandparents coming up for parents' weekend, Amos?"

"What? Oh, yes, they might come up." After a moment he added quietly, "I hope they do."

"What if they don't?" Tommy looked deeply into his friend's face for the agitation that had crept into his voice. "Would you miss them, Amos?" Out of the corner of his eye he could see the lights of the campus sparkling warmly in front of them – soon there would be coffee. He dropped his eyes to the snow at his feet and let his boots lull him with their noisy crunching. A tong-like hand seized his shoulder suddenly, and he turned, feeling the last bit of warmth bleed out into the frigid winter night.

"Maybe I'll miss them, Pendoro, and just maybe I won't. The one thing I'm sure of is that it's not any of your business either way…"

"But, Amos, I…"

"Shut up! Shut up!" His arms flapped awkwardly. "I shouldn't listen to you anyway. You're just like McDougal and the rest, always prying where you shouldn't be. My grandparents have done a lot for me. They brought me up and taught me to love Jesus, didn't they? God!" Amos' entire body shuddered, and a low moan rose from the depths of his soul. He pointed an accusing finger at Tommy, and his eyes filled with fire. "And you, sinner! The gifts of the Kingdom will be forever withheld from you. You are damned!"

"And you are saved," Tommy said quietly.

"Yes! Saved!" His arms gathered the stars to his chest and crushed them. "I have trodden the road of salvation by denouncing the sins of my age, but to no avail. They ignore me. The New Jerusalem awaits those who…"

"You hate them for what they've done to you, don't you?" They stood face to face. A sharp wind lapped their ankles with a blast of glittering ice motes. "You hate them, but you're not to blame, Amos – even for that. There's still time to learn. Surely there's still time to learn."

Rage crossed Amos' face and abruptly gave way to tears. He began to sob loudly. Gentle words came to Tommy's lips, but he restrained them and watched Amos turn and walk away from him toward the campus. He watched the shrinking figure pass under one streetlamp and then another, watching the lamplight shine and die and shine again on his friend's back bent with the sins of the world. The arched lampposts were martyrs' gallows, and Amos was going off to find his own. Under a radiant cone far away he turned and cupped his hands. The rising wind brought his words to Tommy in icy whispers:

"You're a fool, Pendoro! An arrogant fool!"

But now he was dead. Tommy had met his grandfather when

he had come for Amos' things, a sallow thin-lipped man with grizzled sideburns and a rust-colored moustache. He had directed the movers with grim authority, standing at the head of the stairs like an aging sea captain directing the abandonment of his own ship. His dark, withered hands clinging to the wooden railing became by slow degrees indistinguishable from the stained wood which they grasped so firmly. He was a dark old man. Tommy had watched Rolfe approach him timidly to offer his condolences. In the shadow of Amos' doorway he listened.

"Mr. Kirk? My name is Tom Rolfe, and speaking for the rest of us, I'd just like to say…"

"He was a bastard," the old man whispered. They listened to the shouts of the movers below them; a bird fluttered noisily in a rain gutter nearby. Rolfe fell silent. A window directly across from them framed a late winter sky, and Tommy, moving out of the shadows into the hallway, studied the two silhouettes: one young and the other old, one full of hope and the other having squandered his hopes on visions of the infinite. "He was a bastard all right, born out of wedlock like the beasts of the field." He raked his throat and let a string of spittle fall to a step below them. He spoke as if short of breath.

"His grandmother and I expected more from Amos. We certainly didn't expect *this*. We had misgivings about the adoption, and I guess we should have listened to our better instincts. He was godless, just like his mother. A child like that carries the mark of the Devil to his grave." He turned and for the first time considered the young man standing beside him. "And to what denomination do you belong, young man?"

Through the window Tommy had watched the blue-black layered clouds ascending endlessly into the heavens. He turned away…

Above him the stars stretched like glittering dust across the firmament. *No, his Answer didn't lie there, either. Yet so eternal, so beautiful. And so deceptively constant.* He walked on.

"Think of gods as objects of gratitude." The room tilted giddily. The pub was full of students and music. Finch and McDougal sat across from him, clenching beer mugs and scowling at him. "How many times have you walked through a quiet forest somewhere and sensed a power moving in

everything you saw or heard or touched, tasted, or smelled, and said to
yourself, 'If only someone would step out from behind a tree and say, "I'm
responsible for all of this – I created everything you see around you now,"'
just so you could embrace him and just say, 'Thank you. Thank you very
much!'? Have you ever felt that way? I can understand why there were so
many pastoral gods in the Greek pantheon: a rustic setting is where one feels
the supernal presence the most keenly." The room began to spin end over
end. McDougal leaned across the table and clamped his hand tightly across
Tommy's mouth.

"You're boring the shit out of us, Pendoro, and you're scaring the chicks
away. Just shut up for a while, OK?" Two coins rolled across the table into
Tommy's lap. "Shut up, and go get me another beer."

He grinned at the sidewalk. The ragged cuffs of his trousers
flapped noisily against his legs. A thick smell of compost drifted
across his path, and he drew it deeply into his lungs, exhaling
slowly. It was a good smell, a rich fertile earthy smell, like
manure. He was nearing the edge of the campus, and the old
buildings squatted around him in the darkness like tolerant old
men, speaking of the years that had passed between them.

Decay – they can speak only of decay. Damp decaying crumbling brick
and mortar and cloistered old men and women mouthing tired words for
those who will pass into other lives. Vapid, jejune, insipid, dull, flat, bland
– devoid of qualities that make for spirit and character.

"I will not go," he said aloud. "It has continued far too long.
No one can make me go."

A mob of jabbing fingers pushed him back against a coarse wall. Boys
his age threw arms and legs against his midsection. They fell back, and he
sagged to the floor of the locker room. Their leader's head hung before him
like a pustulent jack-o'-lantern; the others leaned toward him in the back-
ground like stout trees.

"Stand up, you weak puke."

"I can't. And you can't make me."

Their callow insults passed out of his hearing meaninglessly, but the full
weight of their eyes passing over his thin weak limbs terrified him. His
vision reeled uncontrollably. He had been drawn mindlessly into a situation
pre-ordained, one over which he had no control – he was the victim of a
perverse turn of mind. Walking down the narrow corridor, he had anti-
cipated the curved backs leaning insolently against the lockers, waiting.

They had given their allegiance to a thick-lipped arrogance.

And he was there to serve a larger purpose.

Tommy stepped from concrete to asphalt. To his right a dull red fence slunk silently into the darkness. The campus was now behind him. Ahead lay houses and, farther beyond, pasture land. He shook his head.

A larger purpose? Palimpsests of images of ideas of concepts of abstractions of perceptions. The scop of the estranged Clifton, keeper of the wordhoard. And what next?

An image of a thin ascetic bent over brittle yellow pages appeared to him. He dismissed it, but others appeared in its place: an empty classroom, fingers smeared with chalk dust, a stooped professor with a long white beard, pigeons huddled on a snowy window ledge. He jerked his head more violently to rid himself of the puzzling images. *My life surely lies elsewhere.*

He had walked this way before. Once, in the early fall, his dormitory had organized a picnic in a small park in the countryside. His floor was there along with the second-floor girls and a few of the upperclassmen living on the first floor. They had gathered in front of the hall and walked to the park in small groups, some chatting nervously, with others fringing the bolder ones, all strangers. A tall girl with blonde hair chattered among the rest, speaking vigorously and emphasizing her idle points with forced gestures. His eyes fell and remained on her: her heart was not in her words.

He drifted slowly toward her group so that he could listen more closely. Her name was Susie – Susie Quent. Surely she was just going through the motions. She sensed his eyes and turned occasionally to meet his gaze. She was very pretty. Here was one perhaps to whom he could confide all of his long-concealed dreams and hidden yearnings; here was one who might understand his stifled spirituality and his as yet unrealized artistic aspirations.

And of course, he had considered as an afterthought, *she is also very pretty.*

Later in the afternoon McDougal had dared Susie to slide down a spiral slide headfirst on her chest, and she had arrived at the bottom laughing, with her hair cascading into her dangling arms. Her childlike joy was contagious, and Tommy laughed too.

She raised herself carefully, with dignity, and brushed her hair back from her face. She stopped laughing suddenly and regarded him then with an expression of betrayal that he had never been able to understand. He detected in her eyes a bitterness not unlike his own, a discontentment with life matching his. And yet the look she had given him disturbed him deeply, a look so bereft of compassion that he had felt compelled to look away. A spiritual void seemed to reside in those laughing, bitter, empty eyes.

He now came in sight of another park: Mollens. *Prentiss.* Playground equipment protruded from a muddy field into the attenuated glow of moonlight, thin tendrils of diffuse light soothing his eyes with its warm tumescence. He concentrated on the night: the webbed trees against the milky moonlit clouds, the pleasant yellow glow given off by the passing houses, scattered leaves skittering across the sidewalk, the suspiring life surrounding him in the darkness. They pulled at him and awakened in him an indefinite longing: he was lonely. His steps rang out flatly against those houses which contained in each a vibrant life of its own. He did not belong: as a student, his societal niche was as yet undetermined; as a suspended student, it was virtually non-existent. The others he knew – McDougal, Clifton, Landau, Munro, Finch – would go on to seek more concrete rewards. A misfit, he would be left with nothing to show for his efforts but a handful of ashes. His father's exhortations came to mind: perhaps it was not too late to change his life. He would return home, get a part-time job, and return to school in the fall as an accounting student. His success would be assured, and the change of heart would be lauded on both sides of his splintered family.

No.

He would secure a job with a high potential for upward mobility, marry into a family with traditional Judeo-Christian values, have two children, and settle down to an existence of relative ease and comfort *sine cura.*

No!

But what then? What are the alternatives?

He hurried his steps as if to escape his frenzied thoughts, and his loneliness returned with renewed force. The road ahead wound through the light into dark distant fields. A grotesquely buxom image of Susie Quent shaped itself out of the indistinct shadows and titillated him relentlessly. It danced and fled and returned again, a symbol of fecundity and desire. Lust singed his loins and rose to grapple clumsily with the outrage he had so carefully preserved. She had found favor with another, Clifton, actually playing up to him for the single apparent purpose of spiting both Tommy and Ruth Hager, her hated roommate. And she had loathed Clifton's company to such a degree that she had finally broken off the relationship after a few weeks, estranging not only Clifton but also Ruth, McDougal, and himself in the process. She too was alone now. He had not understood her silent brooding after their single night together or her obvious in-difference to the other boys she had approached and entangled. She had merely tolerated Clifton's puerile machismo for reasons which still remained unclear to him. *Clifton.*

They sit disconsolate
Side by side
Man and woman
His sharp hands tearing tired thighs
Her lips taut and tightening
Like an enduring bowstring.

I saw, I saw:
With face averted she relinquished all.
I saw her weeping eyes.

It was a scrap he had written after the night when he had lost his virginity, an early spring night a year earlier. He had been studying quietly at home in his room when his father kicked his door open suddenly and staggered in, clutching a half empty whiskey bottle.

"Hey, boy!" he slurred. He slashed one of Tommy's books to the floor. "What the hell are you doing in here, boy? Playing with yourself?"

Tommy laced his fingers behind his head and leaned back in his chair against the wall. He said nothing. He would ignore his father, and his father would go away. He closed his eyes and immediately felt a hand strike his jaw sharply. He looked up to see his father leaning heavily against his desk, preparing to strike him again. His cheek stung.

"You smug little son of a bitch. You listen when your father is talking to you." The hand fell again and again. "I didn't raise you to ignore your own father."

Tommy stood up and faced him. His father had struck him – he had done nothing, and his father had struck him. He flew at the man in front of him and lashed at him blindly until his father collapsed under the force of his blows.

"Don't ever hit me again, man. Never again." He choked and began to cry. He clenched and unclenched his hands uselessly, straddling the now motionless body. "You had it coming to you, you old bastard." He fell to the floor and buried his face in his father's shoulder, choking on his tears. "You old bastard." He rose and left to meet the girl, to lose his virginity, to become a man. But in whose eyes?

Father.

There were fewer houses now – he was nearing the edge of town. Looking back he could see the campus lights drenching the small world around it with its weak bone-colored pallor. Ahead lay an endless expanse of uncultivated fields. The last houselight passed by him, and he turned from the asphalt onto a dirt road. A train whistle blew in the distance.

The car was dark where his pencil scratched, dark metal rails shouting "tommy flanders tommy flanders tommy flanders" at the late August night. A cigarette burned nearby. His pencil pivoted awkwardly:

> *The night had settled beneath their feet*
> *Before it coiled and leaped over the river.*

No. "Reared."

> *Before it reared and leaped…*

Her voice had bidden him farewell over the sound of hissing brakes. "Goodbye, Mama. Where's Father?" A cough nearby, sleepy rustling.

"Bye-bye, Tommy." The poem twisted and turned on itself in the

darkness, a wolf-bitch devouring her own young. His girlfriend's voice on the phone, soft, sad. "Goodbye, Tommy. I'll miss you. Will you ever think about me?"

Nor had his many failures…

"Failings…" The poem wiggled and squirmed on the page like a lanced worm. Done.

> *The night had settled beneath their feet*
> *Before it reared and leaped over the river.*
> *The older man knew the life that lay behind him now*
> *And the life beside him created in his own image,*
> *Nor had his many failings been forgotten*
> *In the heat of the summer evening.*

> *"Father?" whispered the boy.*
> *"Hush now," he said. "Watch the river."*

> *He cupped his thoughts in his hand*
> *And scattered them over the water.*

> *They sparkled softly beneath them,*
> *A river of stars.*

Hush, Father. Be still.

Since he had walked beyond the outskirts of town the moon had emerged from behind a bank of clouds to bathe both heaven and earth in its soft ivory brilliance. Insects whirred and chirped in the ditches beside him, and cattle slept peacefully in the bleached fields. Their nearness aroused in Tommy an inner serenity that had not existed before.

Like Prentiss, he would not return. They did not perceive his eccentricities for what they truly were: manifestations of a fertile, gravid genius. He possessed the artist's temperament – he would detach himself completely and forever from that society which had failed to understand him. As Clifton's scop, their deeds, both foolish and meritorious, would become grist for his creativity. He would sing in their halls and be tolerated; he would walk their fields and drink from Orpheus' cup; he would transcend man's base appetites and allow his craft to sustain him. That was to be his lot, that of a Creator, and he would die content in the knowledge that he had served his calling and had not turned away.

In the near distance he could see a girl sitting on a picnic table off to the side of the road. As he drew nearer he realized that this was the same park where his dormitory had picnicked in the early fall. The irony was evident, and he smiled at the childishness of his earlier thoughts.

"Tommy..."

A cool breeze lifted her long, white hair into the moonlight. It was Susie Quent.

"Tommy."

He walked across the road to the table and sat down beside her. The chapel bells clamored somewhere far away, their dying sound sustained and dissipated in the sudden flurry of wind that whipped in random gusts through the trees nearby. His hand fell into hers and remained there. She looked up at him. A single tear sparkled on her cheek, and he kissed it gently.

You arrogant fool. Surely there is still time to learn.

It was cool. They sat silently in the park and listened to the wind in the trees.

Printed in the United States
214110BV00001B/10/P

9 781844 017317